THE HO

CU00665583

Simon Grail

THE HOT POTATO

FETISH WORLD BOOKS

Chapter One

The man, who went by the name of "The Flogger", swung his lash again and again across the lovely, naked, bound body of his captive. Except for his black hood and black jackboots, he was as naked as she was and the stiff shaft of his cock bobbed and wagged with every blow he struck.

The muffled screams of the woman known to him only as "Crystal" were soaked up by the soundproof walls of his play room. She was bound to a metal X-shaped cross, the padded centre of which pressed against the small of her back. The cross had an axle through its middle that was fixed at each end to swivel joints mounted on the posts of its supporting frame. Crystal's arms and legs were twisted and bent sharply at the elbows and knees so that they were doubled up under her body and strapped to the back struts of the cross. It almost made it look as though the lower ends of her limbs were missing, leaving only her head and torso. That suited the Flogger perfectly: letting him get closer to her while focusing his attention on her most intimate parts.

Her thighs were spread wide and her hips were pushed forward, lifting her belly outwards so that her back was arched. The front of her body was held down by more straps bound about her thighs, waist and neck. She had a rubber ring gag jammed into her mouth, keeping her lips wide and her teeth bared.

The cross could be flipped and turned about on its mount, so that he could position her head-up or head-down; with her breasts upwards or dangling beneath her with her bottom exposed, or with her widespread thighs and the moist pink gash between them open towards him. He was her total master and he could do more or less he wanted to her, within the terms of his hire agreement with the men who had supplied her.

By now, Crystal's body was a mess, which was also the way the Flogger liked it. However, this was largely an illusion. The rubber lash he was using on her was impregnated with purple ink, leaving lurid slashes across her skin from knees to shoulders. She was still suffering, though. The thongs still stung and burned as they cut into her soft flesh, making it blush, and she yelped and jerked in real pain, dribbling about her gag.

The sight made his straining cock twitch again and he could feel the pressure behind it becoming irresistible. He flipped her into position and rammed it up into her gaping pussy, while still lashing her lovely big breasts, which flattened and bounced and slapped about under his blows. With a grunt of triumph he came inside her, filling her with his hot sperm. He felt her hot slippery vaginal tunnel clench tight about him in response as an orgasm tore through her sweaty body, straining against her straps and making the cross and its frame creak. Then he sprawled on top of her hot bound body, feeling her panting for breath beneath him and rested, perfectly satisfied.

After several minutes, he pulled his now flaccid cock out of her clinging pussy and walked around her body and pushed it through her ring gag into her gaping mouth. Still half dazed, her eyes rolled about as his balls rubbed across her nose while dutifully she licked and sucked him clean. As a final mark of his domination, he wiped his penis dry on her hair.

Now he was satisfied, the Flogger felt a spark of genuine affection for Crystal. He stroked her hot cheeks still stained with her tears. She had been recommended to him by others within the exclusive circle of those with similar specialised interests to his own. She had been expensive to hire but worth every penny. A natural: a genuine submissive masochist.

Crystal was an attractive woman, perhaps in her late twenties, with a well-toned body. Clearly, she looked after herself. Even beaten and exhausted as she was, she had an air of class and style about her: a professional woman, maybe?

It put him in mind of one of those cool, well spoken, smartly dressed woman media presenters, who everybody suspects is steaming hot underneath. Crystal's hotness was beyond dispute. The juices had poured out of her dripping vulva. There were splashes of it on the floor and he could smell it in the air. She had come for real over him: no faking. She got off on being treated like a shameless, hungry sex slut.

He stroked her hair again. 'How did a classy woman like you end up with your pussy for hire?' he muttered, half to himself.

Crystal heard him through the blissful haze of masochistic delight still filling her mind like warm candy floss. I was just going to the airport, she thought, but I never got there…

* * *

The crossroads in the middle of Tilehurst Woods was a useful shortcut to the nearest main road that would take Angela to Gatwick airport and her early flight. At this time of night it should have been deserted, but there was a confusion of headlights flashing ahead of her accompanied by the sounds of several powerful engines. These resolved themselves into the figures of four bikers in leathers and goggles and helmets and chains riding their bellowing, gleaming chrome machines back and forth across the junction, performing doughnuts and wheelies and raising clouds of burnt rubber.

The wild, careless irresponsibility the sight of them represented, so very different from her own orderly lifestyle, made Angela angry. She hit her horn and flashed her headlights at them. Get out of my way, she thought!

But they did not make way. Instead, they broke off from their games and circled their bikes around her car.

This only angered her even more and she leaned out of the driver-side window. 'You're blocking the road! Get out of my way.'

'Going somewhere important, are you?' a big ginger bearded biker asked, pulling up beside her. His eyes were covered by tinted goggles.

She tried to sound reasonable. 'I'm going on holiday and I've got to get to Gatwick to catch an early flight. Now please get out of the way…'

The ginger biker peered into the car. 'Going on holiday alone? A pretty woman like you hasn't got a man to go with her? Or a girlfriend? We're not prejudiced, are we lads?'

A mocking cheer rose up from the other bikers.

'It's none of your business whether I go alone or not,' she snapped. 'Now for the last time, get out of my way!'

He kicked down the support struts of his bike and leaned closer. Suddenly he sounded menacing. 'Nobody tells Big Red to get out of their way!'

Then she realized that the biker on the other side of the car was also leaning into it. She had the windows down for ventilation. Suddenly feeling vulnerable, she pressed the switch to close them, but he held the rising panel of glass down, so the safety cut-out stopped it rising further.

'Somebody wants to get to know you better, Angela,' Big Red said with a grin.

How did he know her name!

For the first time Angela felt real fear. She tried to grab her bag with her phone in it which was on the passenger seat, but the other biker picked it up. As she twisted round and tried to grab it and pull it back, Big Red reached in through her window and took hold of her by her hair with one hand, while with the other he pressed a cloth over her nose and mouth, stifling her scream. A chemical scent filled her sinuses and burned her throat as her desperate intake of breath sucked it down into her lungs... cloying... heavy... dizzy... blackness...

* * *

Angela hauled herself out of the darkness back into the light. Her head was throbbing and spinning and she felt sick and there was a strange taste in her mouth, which was wedged open by what seemed to be a rubber ball that pressed her tongue down. It was threaded onto some elastic cord that cut into the corners of her mouth and pulled her lips back and exposed her teeth. Why had she got a rubber ball in her mouth, she wondered foolishly?

More questions filled her fuzzy mind. How was she standing up when her legs felt too weak to hold her...what was pinching about her neck and arms and ankles... and why was she totally naked?

Filled with a sudden thrill of terror, she groaned and blinked the gum out of her eyes and made them focus.

She was looking down the length of a large room with a stained concrete floor, corrugated sheet iron walls and lattice iron frame roofs beams. Its windows were covered by sheets of translucent plastic through which shone suffused golden morning light. Four motor bikes were parked at one end in front of a set of double doors and beside a big tool cabinet on wheels. Bike parts and chains hung about the walls looking like heavy metal decorations. Under them was a row of mismatched, patched and battered chairs on which lounged three of the bikers who had stopped her in the woods. They still had their helmets and goggles on and were drinking from cans and bottles while watching something involving screeches of tyres, shouts and gunfire on a big flat screen TV hung on the wall opposite.

To one side of them was a large table at which "Big Red", also still goggled and helmeted, sat hunched over a laptop. There was something on the table beside the

9

laptop. It looked like her phone! And he was plugging it into the other machine. What was he doing with it? And how had he known her name?

Angela blinked at the men foolishly, realising they just had to look around to see her naked body. But then of course they had already seen it. They must have stripped her... handling her all over with their filthy hands... Oh God, she thought, trying not to be sick, even as her nipples stood up, what else might they have done to her? Feeling dirty and defiled, she tried to move, to cover herself, but she could not. She twisted her head round to see why.

On either side of her, a pair of scaffolding poles rose out of base plates bolted to the floor to one of the roof beams above her head. A third pole set almost at head height and secured by scaffold couplers crossed between the first two. Her arms were stretched out sideways along this pole to which they had been tied about with loops of bungee cord from wrists to shoulders. Another bungee was looped about her neck, holding her head up. Two more long cords ran inwards from the bases of the scaffolding poles and were wrapped tightly about her ankles, holding her legs apart. She was standing on a black plastic sheet that had been spread out between the upright poles. There was even a short bungee cord threaded through the rubber ball clamped between her teeth, which was hooked together behind her head.

Feebly she squirmed and moaned, tugging at her bonds. But the bungee cords simply absorbed her efforts and then pulled her back into position again. She was totally helpless.

But she had made enough noise to be heard over the racket coming from the television. One of the bikers looked around and nudged the others. They muted the television sound. 'Red... she's awake,' one said.

10

Big Red finished working on her phone and got up and came over to her. She felt herself cringing inwardly as her cheeks burned in shame and fear, but she forced herself to gaze back at him defiantly.

'Good of you to join us again, Angela,' he said cheerfully. 'Don't worry, the headache doesn't last long. I've been waiting for you to wake up so I could take some pictures to send to our client. He'll want to be sure you're not damaged before he takes delivery...' He looked her naked body up and down with evident approval and nodded. '... and I think you're worth every penny...'

Angela had a strong, intelligent face, deep keen blue eyes, dark hair, a firm straight nose, high cheekbones and an expressive mouth. She was slender with a well toned body which accentuated her full, heavy natural breasts with perky nipples. She had womanly hips and well-rounded buttocks and a pink, plump-lipped, pussy crowned by a neatly trimmed thatch of brown curls.

All this Big Red was taking in at his leisure, which only redoubled her shame.

She snivelled and shook her head and tried to speak back to him around her gag, but it was pinning her tongue down. He held up a phone and snapped pictures of her from every angle, including a close-up of her distraught face. Then he made a call.

'Marquis?' he asked cheerfully. 'Good morning, Big Red here. We've got the special item you wanted... Yes, it was today. Sending you pictures now... got them? Yes, that one. As you can see, it's fresh and undamaged... Yeah, it was just where we thought it would be. The item's transport has been taken care of. We'll dispose of it when things cool down. So, where shall we arrange a meet so we can hand it over?'

The "item" was her, Angela realized in despair. She had been reduced to a thing: a piece of merchandise...

11

Up until now, Big Red had been talking confidently, but suddenly he frowned.

'What do you mean, it's not as attractive as you imagined… How long since you last saw it … Eh? You've never seen it uncovered before…? You never even had spy pictures taken… Well maybe you should have done. Anyway, look at it now: worth every penny… You think it looks cold… No, it's hot… Yes, I can prove it, hold on…'

He turned to the other bikers, who had left the television to gather closer when they heard the tone of his voice change. Despite her terror, Angela realized that with their faces covered by beards, goggles and helmets, and dressed in similar worn sets of jeans, leather jerkins, big boots and chains, they appeared to be totally anonymous and interchangeable. The only variation between them was that they wore differently coloured bandannas tied about their necks.

'True,' Red said to the one wearing the blue bandanna, 'get the pussy drill screw out. The buyer wants a demo…'

"True" went to the equipment locker and came back with a cordless power drill that has a huge rubber screw shaft on its end.

'Watch this,' Red said into the phone, and then pointed it at Angela.

True knelt between Angel's spread legs and pushed the huge shaft up into her vulva. The drill began to purr and then judder as it moved into hammer mode. Angela's eyes bulged in horror and she screamed and bit on her gag as the thing entered her intimate cleft, churning against her flesh, parting her labia and making her lips shiver.

She tried to pull away from it, but there was no escape. It was so huge and menacing that she imagined for a moment it tearing a hole in her, but of course it was in fact penetrating a hole that was already there. Its rubber sides gave slightly as it churned into her vagina, making her lower belly vibrate from within.

Half the terrible shaft had disappeared inside when she gasped and threw back her head rolled up her eyes with helpless delight. The relentless vibrations were pummelling the root of her clitoris from within: so powerful that she could not deny them. Despite her terror she was responding to its overwhelming presence, smothering the rational, revolted side of her.

Her natural shame was pushed into the shadows by a sudden animal lust for pleasure she had never known before. Her eyes fluttered and she drooled about her gag as wave upon wave of raw delight flowed up through her body filled her mind. It was obscene, insulting and crude and… and incredible! Dimly she was aware of her nipples swelling up into brazen crowns.

True pulled the drill out of her wet slot for a moment, splattering her juices over her thighs, to rub its shiny slick wet spinning shaft over her breasts and hard nipples, making them throb fit to burst. Then he thrust the terrible, growling, whirring shaft back inside her, and she squeezed desperately.

He began to pump with his whole arm, adding to its impact. Her lower belly was bulging and sucking upon it. She longer cared if it would do her any damage. A wonderful, terrible pressure was building up inside her. It was like the pre-orgasmic thrill she got using her favourite vibrator, except that it was ten times worse… or better!

Her hips were grinding back and forth as if she was riding the churning pussy drill. She was impaling herself again and again…

Angela shrieked about her gag she came over the drill, squeezing its spinning shaft so tightly that for a few seconds the motor growled as it fought against her grip. Pleasure fireworks burst in her brain. There was nothing else but her body and the thing inside her, driving on and on into a glorious sunset…

Then she went limp to the sound of the bikers applauding her lustful display.

True pulled the pussy screw out of her slot, dripping with her juices and held it up in front of the phone's camera.

Big Red put the phone to his ear again. 'There, you see. That's the hottest thing I've ever seen… What, it's not responsive enough! But it came… No, you can't… five hundred for our trouble… But you were going to pay… I see, take it or leave it… Doesn't look like we've got any choice, does it… What do we do with it… put it back… just like that? Hello… Hello?'

He switched off the phone and scowled at Angela and then the other bikers. 'No deal. Looks like we're stuck with her,' he said.

Chapter Two

Only half conscious, still wrapped in a blissful post-orgasmic haze which was temporarily keeping her fear and shame at bay, Angela listened to the bikers discussing her with a curious detachment.

'A fucking five hundred for a night's work,' the biker wearing a yellow bandana exclaimed. 'That's an insult! We were going to get five thousand for delivering her. That was the deal!'

'And now it's not,' said Big Red. 'Bloody idiot! He never had her checked out properly. Never screwed her, never even got spy pictures taken of her in the bathroom to see her starkers! Now he decides she's not what floats his boat and that's that.'

'But he must be loaded,' said the green bandanna-clad biker. 'He could afford to pay us full whack!'

'Maybe that's how he got loaded,' said True, 'by not paying when he didn't have to. He knows we can't do anything about it.

'That's rich men for you,' said Big Red bitterly. 'They order a new toy and change their minds before it's even delivered!'

The green biker took hold of Angela's hair and lifted her lolling, flush-cheeked and tear-stained head up, as if presenting exhibit A. 'He thinks this is unresponsive and not attractive?' He scooped his fingers through Angela's aching pussy, making her shudder, and then held them up wet and sticky for all to see. She burned in shame and confusion. 'Look at that! Pure cool smart class on the outside with a steaming hot pussy that cums over the drill first time out. Who could ask for more?'

'Apparently he could,' said the yellow biker moodily. 'No accounting for taste…'

Dimly, in that small still detached and observant part of mind, it occurred to Angela that they all sounded

15

better spoken than outward appearance would suggest. And were those beards too thick and bushy to be true…

As she tried to clear her thoughts, the warm pink blissful cocoon that had been insulating her melted away and cold terrifying reality began to flow back in bullet points…

She had been kidnapped!

Angela tried not to give into the sucking dread threatening to swallow her up…

She was tied up and naked!

She'd heard stories of modern day slavery, of course, but she never really believed she could experience such things herself…

She had been violated!

It was something that happened to other people far away, not just a few miles from her own home…

She had cum over a power drill with a rubber screw dildo on its end in front of four bikers and a strange man on the end of the telephone!

And that was almost the worst thing of all, because it made no sense! Yes, she used vibrators on herself, but she could never respond like that. But then her body had never been out of her control before. She hadn't been able to help herself. The proof lay in the splatters of her juices on the black plastic sheet between her spread feet.

'So, what do we do with her now?' True asked.

The terrifying implications of that question stirred Angela into a frenzy of moans and struggles as she tried to speak around the gag filling her mouth. The bikers all turned to look at her for the first time as if she was a person and not a piece of merchandise.

'Sorry about all this, Angela,' Big Red said apologetically, as if genuinely concerned that they had provided her with a substandard service. 'It wasn't meant to happen like this. Right now, we should be packing you up for a little trip to hand you over to your new owner. Only he seems to have changed his mind…'

She was shaking her head frantically, her eyes wide in disbelief. The way he said it so matter-of-factly, it was impossible to take in.

'Oh yes, it's true,' Red assured her. 'Somebody who met you through your work or something, wanted to have you as his sex toy. We don't know his real name, of course, he just called himself "The Marquis". He hired us to snatch you.'

She shook her head again. No!

'Yes. He knew all about you... well, almost all as it turns out. You're twenty-eight and you work for the Hawthorn Leas Advertising Agency. You live at 27B Gravesdean Drive in Chidford, you're unmarried and you have no boyfriend at the moment. You also go on holiday alone. That was your Achilles heel, which is why we took you on the way to the airport. You're meant to be away for three weeks, coming back on the twenty-fourth, right? None of your friends or family expects too many chatty messages from you during that time because that's not your style. Any questions about you not taking your flight or arriving at the holiday villa you booked will go through your phone and that's now connected to a clever computer program which has read all your texts and phone messages and knows your personality and writing style and will take care of it just like you would. For three weeks, nobody will miss you.

'That's long enough for you to be conditioned by specialists – not us because we're just snatchers – into loving your new master like a perfect slave. Expensive, that kind of treatment. Not many masters go that far, but then he could have afforded it - even if he couldn't afford to pay us! Anyway, the plan was you'd come back from your "holiday" saying you'd met somebody special who wanted you to live a private life with him. You'd leave your job and drop out of sight and nobody would ever know the truth.'

17

Angela shook her head feebly, feeling as if she was going to be sick. Somebody had found out all that about her and had planned her kidnapping and wanted to make her his brainwashed sex slave… and then he had rejected her!

'You see, you're not the first woman we've snatched to order, and you won't be the last,' Big Red said. 'Only this time, whoever took such a fancy to you has changed his mind. It took a few weeks to set the operation up. Maybe he saw another pretty girl he wanted more and forgot about you. But that's the way with bloody rich people. Don't care about the little man who has to work for a living…'

The other bikers were nodding in sympathy, looking hard done by. What about her, she raged inwardly?

'So what do we do with her?' the green biker asked. 'Knock her out again and put her back in the woods in her car?'

Angela nodded frantically.

'Its light now,' the yellow biker pointed out, gesturing at the windows. 'Can't risk moving her car in daylight. We'll have to keep her here for the rest of the day.'

'We've wasted enough time on her as it is,' True said. 'I don't want to spend even more of it putting her back where we found her for nothing.'

'In any case she'd talk as soon as she was free,' green pointed out. 'Even if she couldn't identify us, we'd have to keep low for a while. We'd lose even more money!'

Angela was now shaking her head. No, no, she wouldn't talk, she thought, aware of how pitiful that made her seem and not caring. She just wanted to be free of this nightmare!

'We can't do anything until this evening so let's get some sleep and think about it fresh,' Big Red said.

Angela gaped at him in horror. They were going to keep her like this all day!

'Well if we don't have to keep her clean for the bloody Marquis anymore, can we at least have some fun with her?' True asked.

Angela went cold inside.

'Yeah, why not?' Yellow said. 'Be some compensation at least and it can't do any harm. She's no blushing virgin, after all.'

The others were nodding, all looking at Red, while Angela shook her head frantically.

'All right, as long as we don't mark her too hard,' he declared.

Angela began to buck and twist and moan once again, making the scaffold poling joints squeak. They could not do this to her!

'Looks like she needs a bit a bit of taming first,' True said.

'Well that's all part of the fun,' said Yellow.

'Shall I get out the tenderizers?' Green asked.

'Yeah, they should do it,' said Red.

Angela was gurgling in fear and anger about her gag. Red patted her head, and then playfully cupped and squeezed her breasts.

'You can't blame us for wanting to have a bit of fun with you, Angela. You were not good enough for our client and you lost us some money. Don't worry, we're not going to mess with your mind like his brainwashers would have done, but we are going to make you beg to please us with your pretty body…'

While he was speaking, Green had brought out some items from the tool chest and handed them out. They had wooden handles with fifty centimetre lengths of thin rubber cut from the rims of old bike tyres nailed to them, turning them into lashes.

At the sight of them Angela froze. No, they couldn't…

19

'Here's how it works,' said Red, as the men spread out to encircle her. 'We're going to beat you until you cry, which is always fun to see, and then keep on until you beg us to stop hitting you and start screwing you. It's as simple as that. Your choice how much you suffer first and how soon you swallow your pride...'

The four lashes swished through the air and cracked against her body. Angela screamed as the rubber thongs rasped across her flesh. They swished and cracked again and again, embracing the contours of her body. The thongs curled almost lovingly about her breasts and back and belly and buttocks and around her thighs and up between her spread legs; stinging and burning as they did. Her buttocks clenched and her breasts shivered and bounced as they were beaten back and forth and then flattened. Her hard nipples stood up masochistically, only to be driven into their soft supporting globes again and again. The thongs rasped through the cleft of her buttocks and the furrow of her pussy, smacking the throbbing nub of her clitoris.

Angela screamed and sobbed and dribbled and jerked against the bungee cords binding her to the horizontal scaffold pole, which made the uprights shake. Her knees turned frantically inwards and then outwards she strove to pull her thighs together and conceal the terrifying exposed and vulnerable pouting mound of her pussy. But always the elastic cords pulled her back into position again. There was no escape from the terrible pain and shame and fear, even as her body was becoming a single pink blush from knees to shoulders, criss-crossed by deeper scarlet slashes.

Then she felt something beyond the pain and shame as her body once again began responding perversely. Even as she stung and burned, her nipples were hard and her pussy was dripping with juices which the thongs were smearing across her lower belly and the insides of her thighs. She was becoming intensely aroused! No, it

20

wasn't possible, she couldn't be ready to cum again, not after being treated like this. Pain and excitement swirled about each other in her dizzy mind.

An extra hard thrash of a lash up between her legs ripped through her pussy and sent such an intimate jolt of pain through her that it caused her to lose bladder control. A stream of hot pee spurted out of her over the black plastic sheet beneath her feet. She burned in shame and yet thrilled at the sensation of the urine gushing out of her through her sore swollen pussy.

The bikers laughed at her humiliation.

'Enough!' Big Red said, and the bikers rested their arms.

He examined Angela, lifting her drooping head and looking at her flushed and tear- streaked face. Then he felt her simmering breasts and belly and her hot bottom and dripping pussy, wet not just with pee but her intimate juices. 'Interesting,' he said. 'I think we've got a real masochist here, lads…' Then he pulled out her gag. 'You can have more of the same, or you can beg us to screw you,' he told Angela.

She felt the desperate need inside her that the beating had aroused. It was terrifying and beyond explanation but it had to be quenched somehow. She heard herself saying. 'P… please, screw me…'

'All of us?'

A gang bang! A filthy, revolting suggestion that made her nipples throb. 'Yes… yes, all of you…'

'You heard the lady, lads,' Red said.

They pulled out something that had been resting against the wall behind her out of the line of sight. It was a single mattress inside a shallow wooden frame covered with plastic sheeting. The frame had eyebolts screwed to it and chains and straps and more bungee cords…

They untied her from the scaffold poles and she dropped to her knees hardly able to stand. Her numbed

21

arms hung loosely by her side. Every part of her burned and ached. Big Red flicked his tenderiser across her back, making her flinch.

'Get your head down and kiss our boots and beg each of us to screw you properly,' he told her. He stood in front of her. 'You know my name…'

Trembling, sick with shame, Angela bent her head and kissed the shiny toecaps of his leather boots. 'P… please s… screw me… Big Red…'

As she looked back up at him with tear filled eyes, she saw the bulge growing in the front of his jeans.

'Now True Blue…'

She bent over the next set of boots. 'Please screw me, True Blue…' she begged sincerely, looking up at another pair of bulging trousers.

And so in turn, humiliatingly, she kissed the boots of "Mellow Yellow" and "Mean Green," who were equally aroused by her attention. It was so degrading and yet her nipples were hard and excitement. It could not be happening. She was a respectable independent enlightened woman! It must be a nightmare: a dream as unreal as their alliterative assumed names. She had slipped into a fantasy world of secrets, suffering and lies. Then Big Red's tenderiser smacked across her back again, reminding her that it was all too real.

'Now get on the mattress and spread yourself out!'

Unsteadily Angela clambered onto the mattress and lay on her back spreading her arms and legs wide. The bikers buckled straps about her wrists and ankles and then turned her legs outwards, exposing her pale, thong-strapped insides of her thighs, and bound bungee cords about her knees, holding them down against the mattress.

Then they stripped off their boots and trousers until they were naked from the waist down, sporting straining erections. They stood over she and she looked up at the four shafts that would soon be inside her. They still had their goggles and helmets on. She would never see their faces. That only made it more exciting...

No, she could not mean that. But right now, riding some wave of perversion, part of her did. 'Please,' she said, pitifully lifting her hips.

Big Red had her first, lying on top of her, flattening her hot, sore stinging breasts and driving the breath from her even as he pounded into her. She squeezed tight about him, not thinking just responding. Imagine it was a fleshy vibrator inside her; imagine all this was just a crude fantasy...

Big Red came, spurting his seed deep inside her, and she gushed over him. The intense pulse of pleasure as her loins burst almost wiped her mind.

Distantly she was aware of the weight being lifted from her body as Big Red pulled out of her. Her pussy was wiped clean, and then True Blue took his place inside her...

* * *

It was sometime later. Angela lay sprawled on the mattress, unable to move or think, aware of her aching empty pussy and a sticky wet pool under her buttocks.

'She's fucking amazing!' Mellow Yellow was saying. 'She's got to be worth something to somebody!'

'Maybe she is,' Red said thoughtfully. 'We'll work on it. Meanwhile, let's get some sleep...'

Red pushed Angela's gag ball back in and bound a blindfold strap over her eyes, and they left her lying on her own shameful outpourings.

Chapter Three

It didn't take long for the glow of perverse pleasure and gloriously satisfied need to drain from her and be replaced by acute shame and confusion. Angela squirmed feebly on the wet plastic sheet that clung to her back and buttocks. She couldn't imagine how she had responded that way. It had almost been as if it was happening to another person who had somehow taken over her body. Now she felt revolted, filthy and violated. She just wanted to go home!

But she was still a helpless prisoner of the bikers. She was going nowhere unless they allowed it. For the next three weeks, anything might happen to her and nobody would know. That was the downside of leading an independent life. If the program they were using on her phone was sophisticated enough, then nobody would miss her.

But even acute self pity, fear and rage had its limits. At some point, sheer exhaustion claimed her and she slid into a fitful sleep.

* * *

Angela was roused by her blindfold being removed. She blinked and saw Big Red looking down at her. How long had she slept? Brighter white light shone through the windows.

'We're going to clean you up and give you something to eat,' he told her. He held up his tenderiser. 'If you misbehave you get another beating, understand?'

She nodded meekly.

She was freed from the mattress. Her hands were cuffed behind her back and a heavy leather dog collar buckled about her neck and linked to a heavy chain leash. She was led unsteadily through a back door into a tiny lobby where there was a toilet and basin. She was made to sit on the toilet to relieve herself. She shuddered as her wastes passed out of her abused

24

orifices. Big Red wiped her bottom clean, then she was roughly washed with cold flannels and hair was combed. Nobody had ever done such intimate things for her since she was a child. It only accentuated how helpless she was now.

Back in the main room, she was made to kneel in front of the row of ragged chairs where the bikers sat and they fed her sandwiches. She ate with her cheeks burning under their frank, knowing, semi-amused gaze, which even seemed to shine through their goggles. Mellow was holding a camera, filming her as she took food from their hands.

'We want to have something to remember you by, don't we, Angela?' he said.

She shivered. But her mouth was un-gagged to eat, so she could speak. 'Please,' she said meekly, 'let me go… I won't tell anyone… I promise.'

'And if we do, will that make up for the fee we lost on you snatching?' True wondered.

'We'd be better off finding somebody else to sell you to,' Mean said.

Angela shivered. They really would sell her like an animal… 'I'll pay you!' She blurted out. 'Five thousand pounds, wasn't it? I'll pay you that to let me go.'

They laughed.

'And how would that work?' Red wondered. 'Want our bank account details so you can make a transfer, or will you write us an old-fashioned cheque?'

'I'll pay you cash. I can get it. Cash!'

'And we'll have to collect it from somewhere and the police will be waiting for us!' Mellow said with contempt. 'No, we're going to get our monies-worth out of you from somebody who doesn't mind handling a hot potato. You're good for three weeks at the most, and then, when people start missing you, you'll get to hot to handle. So we've got a pass you on before then.'

'But while we find somebody, we're going to have more fun with you,' Red said. 'And the first thing we're going to do is shave that pretty pussy of yours...'

Angela gaped at him in horror. 'What?'

They laid her on her back across the end of the big table and pulled her legs wide. While the others held her down, Red rubbed shaving gel to her pubic curls and then shaved them off. Angela froze in horror as the blade rasped over her most intimate flesh. But Red had a steady hand and did not so much as nick her. When she was perfectly smooth and hairless, they examined the results, rubbing their big fingers over her pale soft smooth lips.

'I like women with bare pussies,' Mellow said. 'It makes them look so much more vulnerable and helpless.'

'And these are nicely rounded and deep cut,' Mean said appreciatively.

'And it's more hygienic and easier to wipe spunk off it like this,' Blue reminded them virtuously.

They all laughed while Angela whimpered.

Red slapped her cheeks to regain her full attention. 'Like I said, Angela, we're just snatchers so we don't usually keep women around here for long. But when we do and it doesn't matter if we get them a little dirty, we do like to play some games with them. So, we're going to have a go with you on the trestle...'

* * *

It was a heavy wooden trestle with a padded top and sturdy splayed wooden legs with strips of rubber nailed to their ends so they gripped the floor firmly and would not slip. One side of the trestle had pairs of buckled leather cuffs bolted midway down and at the bottom of its legs, while on the other side there were metal curtain rods screwed to the legs' outer faces. Fitted to these with metal rings so that they could slide up and down freely, was another pair of buckled cuffs. The ends of a

26

heavy buckled belt were screwed to the top of the trestle beam. Two short upright lengths of scaffolding pole had been bolted to the ends of the trestle top and stood a little over head height. Their upper ends were connected by a horizontal pole so that it hung parallel with the top of the trestle. A large ring was fitted to the middle of the pole from which hung another bungee cord connected to some device of straps and hooks.

The bikers bent Angela over the trestle and spread her legs with her knees crooked and cuffed them to the trestle at the knees and ankles. The pulled the belt across the small of her back so that her belly was pressed down against the padded top of the beam and buckled her down. Her wrists were un-cuffed and they pulled her arms out in front of her, making her take hold of the lower ends of the curtain rails running down the trestle legs. They buckled the cuffs attached to them about her wrists. Now her lower body was fixed firmly to the trestle, while she could lift her upper torso a little, sliding her hands up the curtain rods as she did so.

The Big Red loosened the bungee cord hanging from the crossbar of the trestle and buckled the device on its end around Angela's head. It was a little like a horse's bridle with straps going over her head and the bridge of her nose and under her chin attached to cheek rings. The head strap had a ring on its top on the crown of her head that was hooked to the bungee cord. Two rubber-sheathed hooks on short elastic cords fastened to cheek rings were jammed into the corners of her mouth, stretching her lips back and wedging her teeth open.

The tension on the bridle bungee cord raised her head to about waist height, forcing her to slide her hands up the curtain rails to brace herself. At that point, the strap across the small of her back held her hips down so that she had to her to arch her back, thrusting her breasts forward. Acutely aware of her helpless exposed posture she felt her nipples popping up.

27

Big Red held her chin in his hands, forcing her to look up at him. With his free hand, he reached down and cupped her trembling breasts and ran his thumb around her hard nipples.

'I think secretly you're enjoying yourself, Angela,' he said with a grin, ignoring her look of dismay. 'Now, we're going to give you another thrashing and then you're going to beg to suck us all off.'

Angela felt sick and dizzy, still not quite believing what was happening to her. So that was why her mouth was wedged open. She had only ever performed fellatio on one boyfriend and she had not liked it and had never done it again. But now she knew she had no choice. She was going to have to beg to pleasure four men with her mouth. It was disgusting... yet why were her nipples growing hard at the thought?

If she was going to do it anyway then why not spare herself some pain? Swallow her pride and beg now. But she could not...

The rubber tread lashes swished and cracked across her thighs and backside. She screamed through her wedged teeth and jerked convulsively against the trestle, making it creak. Tears burned her eyes and ran down her cheeks. Her bottom flesh flattened and rippled and burned. Bent over as she was her pouting bare pussy caught the edge of several blows, sending shocking intimate jolts of pain through her loins. Her pussy responded by throbbing and dribbling a surge of juices that were splattered across her thighs.

Now she could say the humiliating words. 'Awww.... Please... I beg you... eeek... may I s... suck you all off,' she choked out through her stretched lips and wedged teeth.

Her own words horrified her. Had she really been made to say them?

Big Red unzipped his flies and freed his cock. He took hold of the straps binding her head and pulled her open mouth down onto his stiff shaft. It slid over her tongue into the back of the throat. She choked and gasped, trying not to be sick as it penetrated her gullet. Her residual tears dripped onto his shaft. She could taste his maleness while its aroma filled her nostrils. Then he began to jerk her head down onto him. She felt the straps tighten about her head as the bungee cord from which her bridle was supported was stretched and then snapped back again.

She was coughing and spluttering and snatching in a lungful of air around his pumping shaft whenever she could. He was using her throat brutally, as he would her vagina. It was so crude and cruel... and yet her pussy was getting hot and swollen and wet.

Big Red grunted and spurted his sperm down her throat and then held his cock in her mouth so she had to swallow it down.

He pulled out of her and Mean took his place, ramming his stiff shaft between her lips...

* * *

When she had finally and shamefully served each one of them, they gave her some water to drink.

Red examined her burning bottom and wet groin, rubbing his fingers through her hot bare wet slot.

'So, maybe you like a bit of rough treatment after all, Angela?'

Now the strange compulsion had left her she shook her head. No, it had been an aberration! She could not really enjoy it being treated like this.

They bound a strap about her eyes, blindfolding her, and then they left her alone with the taste of their sperm lingering in her mouth. She felt dizzy and sick and angry and ashamed, but most of all she felt frustrated. The truth was she wanted to cum! Of course she hated what they done to her, but she couldn't help responding to it. But that wasn't the same as liking it or wanting it. It was... it was... something else!

After an hour perhaps, they came back to her. The blindfold strap was removed and Big Red slapped her cheeks.

'Now you're going to beg us to screw your pretty bare pussy, Angela.'

Angela felt a terrible thrill course through her as the same argument ran though her mind. She had no choice. They were making her do this. They could have her even if she didn't beg. If she didn't beg then they might be even crueller to her. No point in bringing down unnecessary suffering on herself, was there?

Then she heard herself say defiantly. 'No! You'll have to beat me first.'

'As you like. On your tits this time...'

They took their turns to stand in front of her and beat her breasts. The terrible tread lashes swished and cracked against her breasts while she flinched and yelped and twisted her head from side to side, screwing up her eyes as the blows swished under her chin and smacked against her soft flesh. It was even more painful than her bottom being beaten. Her soft breasts flattened and jumped and leapt and shivered under the blows while she strained against her bound hands, clenching them about the rails screwed to the trestle legs, frantically sliding them up and down as she squirmed and tried to pull away in a futile attempt to avoid the blows, while her head twisted and jerked from the elastic tether that held it upright. But there was no escape from the pain. Well, only one escape...

As her breasts were turning into raw pink melons, she screamed. 'P... please will you screw my pussy...'

Once again, each of them took her in turn, kneeling on a padded bench between her legs and clasping onto her upraised buttocks and ramming their shafts up into her smooth wet sex mouth. The impact of their hips against her sore bare bottom made her burning breasts jiggle and sway. She was being used in the most primitive way possible. She was just a tube of flesh that existed for their pleasure alone.

When they had all taken their pleasure, they blindfolded her again. A bucket was pushed between her spread thighs and she emptied herself into it, not only urine but her juices and the clinging dregs of their sperm. Her sore pussy was wiped clean and then they left her alone again.

But now she suspected they were not quite done with her. There was one other passageway they had left to violate, once they had recovered their vitality. She anticipated its ravishment with terror and helpless dark curiosity.

It was a little longer than before, as far as she could judge, when they came to her again. They kept the blindfold on while she felt a rubber tube being pushed up into her anus. Her sphincter clenched instinctively against it, trying to resist, but of course it was useless. Warm water flushed her rectum out so that it fell into the bucket they'd used to collect her pee. Then they wiped her clean. A big finger bearing a dollop of lubricating jelly was pushed up into her bottom and twisted about, greasing her thoroughly. Only then did they remove her blindfold.

'Time for your bum to get a bit of exercise, Angela,' Big Red told her. 'Let's hear you beg for it…'

'You know what you've got to do first,' she said defiantly. 'You've already beaten my boobs and bottom. What part are you going to beat next?'

Unfortunately he had an answer. 'Just your pussy,' Big Red said.

Angela shrieked as the rubber tyre thongs swished precisely up between her spread thighs and smacked full onto the pouting pouch of her sex mouth. The impacts seem to punch the pain right through her body while her flattened and spread labia exposed the hard nub of her clitoris, sheltering in its hot wet depths, to the bite of the treads. Her pussy burned and throbbed in agony.

The shameful words tumbled out of her wedged mouth in an almost incoherent rush. 'Please... eeek... Screw my bottom... owww ...fuck my arse... I want you up my anus... ahhhh... screw my bum... sodomised me... please!'

And they did; each ramming their hard cocks between her sore bottom cheeks, forcing her greased sphincter apart so that it slid down their thrusting lengths. They pounded and grunted and came into her depths. She clung to them as they pulled out of her. The hose was used quickly to flush her clean, and then the next cock took its place.

As the last biker took his pleasure from her bottom, another monstrous orgasm overwhelmed her and she screamed and fainted.

* * *

Angela was only half conscious when they took her to the little toilet cubicle and let her relieve herself properly and then cleaned up. When they brought her back into the main room, she saw the light was fading in the misty plastic covering the windows. She had been their sex slave for nearly a whole day.

They switched on electric lights and fed her some more sandwiches while they sat on their battered chairs and ate pizza. Then they had her kneel in front of them and rested their heels on her back while they watched another noisy video.

'The Marquis was a fool to let this one go,' Mellow declared. 'She's icy cool on the outside but hot slut inside, and you've got to break the ice to get to it, which only adds the fun.'

'Yeah, she's quality all right,' Mean agreed. 'We've got to be able to make some money out of her somehow.'

'I'm working on it,' Big Red promised.

Angela shuddered.

* * *

When they were finished for the night, they pulled out a small cage on wheels with a bit of padding and a blanket on its floor. It was just big enough to hold her if she was doubled up. They cuffed her wrists together again behind her back, put the ball gag back into her mouth and the blindfold strap over her eyes, and pushed her inside it and padlocked it securely. Then they left her alone again.

Angela lay there, burning and aching inside and out, sobbing in quiet despair and disbelief at how she had suffered and what the next day might bring until she fell asleep.

Chapter Four

The next morning, Angela's blindfold was removed and she was pulled out of her cage and taken through to the little washroom to be cleaned up. After a night in the cramped cage and the previous day of bondage and beating, she could hardly stand. Her vagina and rectum felt bruised inside and out and her throat was raw. Every part of her body ached or simmered and she winced as a cold flannel was rubbed over her breasts and bottom and into her groin.

The bikers chuckled at her discomfort.

'You'd hurt less if you hadn't been so stubborn, Angela,' Mellow said.

And it was true! What had she done/

They took her back into the workshop room and fed her more sandwiches. And then she was knelt on the floor while a new device was wheeled out in front of her.

It was a gleaming silver motorbike set on a sheet metal podium. It had no front wheel and its front fork was held upright by tubular metal struts so it could not turn. It is rear wheel rested on a pair of rollers set into the base of the podium. A large flexible hose was plugged into the motorbike's exhaust and snaked away through the back door of the room, making it look a little like the test stand arrangement used to analyse engine performance in a laboratory. What such test machines did not usually have were huge double dildos mounted on their saddles and chains and cuffs fixed to extra bars fitted over their handlebars and footrests. In addition, the double rollers on which the rear wheel of the bike sat were not smooth but patterned with ribs and corrugations.

'Like it?' Big Red asked. 'We only bring it out for special guests. We call it our Silver Scream Racer...'

They un-cuffed her wrists and lifted her up onto the saddle of the bike, guiding the tips of the twin dildos up

34

into her vagina and rectum. She gasped and dribbled about her gag ball as the huge shafts penetrated her, stretching her aching passage ways wide and then plugging them to the hilt. They made her grasp the ends of the T shaped metal bar that had been welded onto the top of the handle bar post and cuffed her wrists to it. From the position her hands were held in, she could not touch the actual handlebars or operate the throttle or brakes. Her feet were pushed down into the rests and straps were bound about her ankles and over her toes, so that she could not operate the clutch lever. Nor could she could get off the strange machine.

'Now you're going to go for a ride,' Big Red said. 'We'll let you off when we think you've cum enough...'

They started the engine, its exhaust being carried away through the hose, and adjusted the throttle and put the motorbike into gear. The rear wheel began to spin, turning the rollers on which it rested. The ribs and grooves of the rollers churned against the treads, setting it bouncing, shivering and twisting wildly.

As it bucked and kicked and slewed from side to side, pivoting about its immobile front fork, it growled and vibrated fiercely, setting Angela's bottom flesh shivering and her breasts trembling. It was like having it animal between her thighs - or else the biggest most powerful vibrator she had ever imagined! The most intense vibrations of course travelled through the twin dildos deep into her body. Her aching sheathes shivered and buzzed and then seemed to turn to liquid.

Desperately she clung to the handlebars to stay upright and squeezed her thighs against the sides of the engine. Even then she was rocked from side to side as the bike's rear wheel slewed about, pushed to and fro by the uneven ribs on the spinning rollers. This only twisted and churned her hips even more forcefully about the vibrating dildos.

35

Mean and True reached forward and between them put the bike into a higher gear. Angela gasped and sobbed and dribbled around her gag ball as the metal monster roared and bucked under her. Her insides were turning to hot sensuous jelly that wanted to be squirted out of her. The nipples on her jiggling breasts were standing up and throbbing hard. The bikers noticed this and laughed and took turns tweaking and stretching on them as she desperately clung to the saddle.

Again the bike was shifted into a higher gear.

Angela screamed about her gag as the machine pounded into her and felt her insides explode. She bounced on the bucking saddle, squeezing and sucking on the twin shafts as they plunged in and out of her and her juices poured out over them and sizzled as they dripped and splattered over the hot engine. Then she collapsed across the roaring machine accompanied by the cheers and applause of the bikers.

* * *

The bikers revived her and gave her some water and then they started her off again on her blissful ride to nowhere. She came twice more. The last time she also wet herself, which brought forth more laughter.

While the pee was still wet between her thighs, Big Red grasped her hair and lifted her limp head so he could peer into her bleary eyes. He pulled out her gag.

'Do you want another ride Angela, or will you beg to give us one?'

'P... please... Sir... will you ride me?' she begged.

They brought out the restraining mattress again. They freed her from the bike and lifted her off it, the dildos coming out of her sticky dripping passageways with shameful sucking pops. Her legs were quite useless and she could not stand. They laid her on the mattress and spread her out and strapped down, and then took their turns to mount her.

As they rode her helpless body, Angela thought dizzily how much she hated them and the mystery "Marquis" for rejecting her. Yet at the same time it was impossible to hate because it could not be true. Part of her still felt detached, as if it was happening to somebody else. She could not have just cum over a phallic motorbike…

And then a massive and all too real orgasm overwhelmed her…

* * *

She must have slept after the quadruple screwing, because the next thing she knew, Big Red was slapping her cheeks to wake her. Once again, the light was fading beyond the misty plastic windows. She was totally numbed and exhausted. She could barely feel her legs or thighs. Even without the straps she could hardly have moved. And yet frighteningly at that moment this seemed entirely proper and right.

Red pulled her gag out and gave her some water. 'We've got a buyer for you,' he announced. 'A man called Raven. He'll be collecting you tomorrow.'

Those few simple sentences shocked her back into full awareness.

'No… please… you can't do this to me… I'm not a thing you can sell!' she sobbed, momentarily feeling terror at the thought of leaving these four men who had abused her so brutally.

'Yes you are, Angela. You're our merchandise. We've got sell you on to make money. Don't worry, Raven's very respectable. He'll take good care of you…'

'Wh… what kind of name is "Raven"?' she choked out.

'The only name you'll know him by. Get this straight: anonymity is your protection and your best chance of seeing your home once more. You can't identify us because you don't know our real names, you've never seen our faces and you don't know where this place is. That's how it's going to be with everybody who handles you. They'll be masked one way or another and you'll only know them by their dungeon names. Because you're a hot potato and can't be kept permanently, Raven may choose to pass you on after a few days. That's up to him. When you finally get too hot, you'll be cleaned up and dumped a long way away where you can make contact with your cosy little world again. And the only reason this will happen is if you have no idea who had you or where you've been, because what you don't know, you can't tell.'

He said it is if that was meant to reassure her. Perhaps it did, in a terrifying way. But still meant she had to survive almost three weeks as a helpless sex slave plaything.

As she lay there trembling, trying to take all this in, Big Red freed her left arm so that he could twist her upper body round. He had an indelible black marker pen in his hand and used it to write carefully on the nape of her neck, above the rim of her collar on the spot normally concealed by the tumble of her hair.

'I've written "THTH by 24th",' he told her. 'That means you'll be too hot to handle by the twenty-fourth of this month. The program plugged into your phone should keep you safe to play with until then. Whoever has you on that day will know they've got to get rid of you.'

She would never know where she was going or who was taking her. That offended her deeply. She had always known where she was going before! But now ignorance meant she would not be a threat to the inhabitants of this dark underworld. While she was in their power, she must learn to accept that. She was no longer in control of her own destiny!

'If it helps, you're going to be anonymous as well,' Big Red said. 'The name Angela Winston stays here.

I've chosen a slave name for you. Sort of suits your cool quality. As far as Raven is concerned, he's buying the lease of a girl called "Crystal".'

Chapter Five

Raven was a tall dark man wearing black trousers, a black hooded sweatshirt, and a Zorro style black fabric mask over his sharp blue eyes. He looked Angela over with careful scrutiny.

She was on display spread-eagled in the scaffold frame once more. The horizontal bar had been raised over her head and her up-stretched arms had been strapped to it, allowing Raven to examine her freely from both sides. Her mouth was again plugged by a ball gag.

While the four bikers looked on anxiously, Raven took Angela's chin in his hands and turned her head from side to side to examine her expression. Then he pinched the flesh of her shoulders and traced the lines of her collar bones. He cupped and squeezed her breasts, stretching them outwards and then pressing them together. He tweaked and stretched her shamefully hard nipples. He ran his hands over smooth slopes of her buttocks and patted and pinched them to see what proportion was fatty padding and what muscle. He squeezed her thighs and stroked her knees and calves. Then he brought his hand up between her legs and rubbed his finger through the soft bare cleft of her pussy. His thumb turned across the hard fleshy nub of her clitoris. Her eyes rolled up and she groaned helplessly, dribbling about her gag.

Her heart was thudding and she squirmed in a futile attempt to avoid his touch. The strange man was handling her like an animal with the prospect of buying her, which was repulsive and degrading and yet somehow so terrifyingly exhilarating.

'Yes, she certainly looks very attractive,' Raven declared, when he had finished his examination. 'But I'm not sure she's worth the money you're asking...'

'She's got class and she's smart and educated,' Red said. 'Listen to how she speaks…'

He pulled Angela's gag ball out of her mouth so it hung over her throat.

'I… I'm meant to beg you to buy me now,' Angela said, her voice trembling with emotion, 'but I'm not going to. You can do what you want about that…'

She tensed, expecting to be punished.

'You're not going to tell me what I'm doing is wrong or threaten me with the police?' Raven wondered.

'Would it do me any good?' Angela asked.

'No,' Raven admitted.

'That's why I didn't waste my breath,' Angela said.

'You see, she's still feisty and defiant,' said Red quickly. 'A real ice maiden on the outside, but a natural sub under that. Of course, she won't admit what she is yet. On a bit of a personal voyage of discovery there, if you know what I mean. But think of the fun you can have breaking her in.'

'She has to pretend to save her pride,' True explained. 'She won't just submit like that. You need to push her hard until she feels she's been brave enough. Then you'll find she's a hot masochistic slut at heart.'

That's not true, none of it, Angela thought fiercely. But she said nothing.

'I see you've played with her already,' Raven commented, riding his fingers over the fading stripe marks on her buttocks.

'She was no innocent virgin when we snatched her, if that's what you mean,' Red said. 'We haven't done anything serious. She's still got plenty of fight left in her.'

Raven looked at Angela. 'If I buy you, will you resist me?'

She gulped. Those few words carried terrifying implications. 'Yes… I will.'

'Until I break you?'

She gulped again. 'Until... I can't take any more and it's better to submit than suffer... but that still won't mean you'll have won! I'm not anybody's sex slave!'

'What's your name?'

'It's... Crystal,' Angela said. She had just spoken her slave name!

Apparently satisfied, Raven pushed her gag back in. Then he looked at the bikers again. 'And she's good until the twenty-fourth?'

'All covered until then, barring accidents.' He gestured at the table where Angela's phone was plugged into the laptop. 'And we'll keep it that way, guaranteed.'

'Look, have some fun with her for a few days and then pass her along,' Mean suggested. 'You'll get your money back on her easily. Probably even make a bit if you can say she's had some training.'

'Trust us, she's a bit special,' Mellow said.

'All right, I'll take her,' Raven said.

Angela shivered. She had just been bought from her kidnappers! She really was a piece of merchandise. The bikers grinned. An envelope changed hands...

Raven pulled a piece of folded black cloth and an eyedropper bottle out of one pocket. The cloth opened up the form a simple eyeless hood. He used the eyedropper to drip a little clear fluid onto it. Then he pulled it over Angela's head.

Breathing through the cloth, heavy soporific chemical fumes filled her nostrils. She whimpered and shook her head, trying to dislodge the hood, but the stuff filled her lungs and everything seemed to grow faint and distant and black...

* * *

The next thing Angela was aware of, apart from the throbbing pain in her head and the nauseating sickness in

42

her stomach, was a stretch of black rubber floor tiles stretching out in front of face.

She was lying huddled up on her side with her cheek resting on the tiles. She still had her ball gag in, but the anaesthetic hood had been removed. Her arms were twisted round behind her back and her wrists were cuffed together. They seemed to be linked to a belt buckled about her waist. There was a kind of chain collar around her neck with another chain tugging on it.

She moved her head slightly and saw a pair of black shoes and black trousers and the feet of a stool in front of her.

'Take your time to recover, Crystal,' Raven said. 'When you're steady enough, get onto your knees…'

She twisted her head round further, taking in her surroundings while breathing deeply and trying to clear head. She was in a large windowless room, perhaps a converted cellar, with a white ceiling and black walls and a flight of stairs in one corner. On another wall was an open shower cubicle and toilet, backed by black tiles. Unidentifiable things comprised of chains and rods and bars were hung about the walls on racks and hooks, together with more recognisable instruments of punishment. Some kind of cage hung from the ceiling in one corner and a chair-like device was set out in the middle of the room.

Where was she? How long had she been unconscious? Had he done anything to her while she slept?

Panic and revulsion flickered in her sluggish mind. She had to face the terrifying reality that for the next three weeks she was going to be a sex slave hot potato, being passed from hand to hand before she burned somebody. No, that would drive her insane! Then she took a deep breath and corrected herself. Angela Winston might have been driven insane, if it was happening to her. But Angela Winston was a

43

respectable woman who had gone on holiday. Crystal was a mysterious woman without a past: a hot-blooded slut who, if she was pushed hard enough, became excited by rough sex as a kind of... a kind of survival mechanism. Yes, that was it! Crystal could survive this ordeal. She already was surviving. Just count the days. Nearly three gone already...

Taking another deep breath and swaying slightly, Angela rolled onto her knees and then straightened up to face Raven. He was holding the other end of her chain leash. He had collared and chained her like a dog. She felt her nipples stirring and standing up at the thought...

He had removed his black sweatshirt to reveal a black shirt underneath but he still had the Zorro mask on, so the upper half of his face was still concealed. And now in his other hand, he held an electric cattle prod.

'Spread your knees so I can see your pussy open wide,' he commanded. 'That's how a slave should present herself in front of her master...'

She was a little slow to respond. He jabbed the twin pronged tip of the prod into her right breast.

She shrieked and jerked in pain as stinging electric needles stabbed into her flesh. The sharp pain had the effect of clearing more of the fug from her brain. Desperately she sat up straight, opening her thighs wide so he could see her shaven sex mouth.

Raven looked her up and down with approval. 'That's more like it. Obedience is everything. You better learn that if you're going to last until the twenty-fourth...'

He got up and jerked on her leash. The chain around her neck contracted, pinching her skin. It was a choke chain leash!

Clumsily, still swaying slightly, Angela stood up.

'Follow at my heel,' he told her.

He walked her around the room a few times, dragging her after him. Now he was treating her just

44

like a dog. But it helped clear her mind and she steadied down.

'Good girl,' he said.

He led her over to the toilet and hung the end of her choke chain leash on a hook above it.

He held up the cattle prod again. 'You don't want me to use this on you again do you?'

She shook her head.

'So you'll do everything I tell you and not make things harder than they need to be?'

She nodded.

'Do you want to be nice and clean again?'

She nodded.

'Then sit on it with your legs wide and empty yourself out,' he commanded.

Trembling she did so, feeling her cheeks burning. For a moment, she was not sure if she could go, and then she realized that she was bursting and it all poured out of her.

There was a coiled hose beside the toilet with a selection of rubber nozzles on the rack above it. He pushed one up inside her pussy and flushed it out; removing the dregs the bikers had left inside her. Despite herself, she felt a flicker of gratitude for that. Then he changed the nozzle and used it on her bottom, washing the solid waste out of her and making her shudder afresh.

When she was clean inside, he led her over to the shower cubicle and hung the handle of the choke chain on another hook high up on its back wall. There was a shelf holding soap, scrubbing brushes and shampoo and a rail holding fresh towels.

'No talking unless I give you permission, you understand?'

She nodded.

He unbuckled her gag strap and removed her wrist cuffs and belt. Then he turned on the shower. She

45

washed and shampooed herself clean under his eyes, burning with shame and quaking with fear and yet revelling in being clean once more. If only you could wash away bad memories as easily. No, those were Angela's memories. This was all happened to Crystal...

When she was dry, with only her hair still a little damp, he led her over to the device in the middle of the room.

It was a kind of open frame chair with a high back but without a seat, made of black painted scaffolding poles bolted and clamped together. Its front legs were spaced much wider apart than its back ones and all were twice as long as normal, raising it up almost like an adult highchair. There was a wooden step in front of it, while underneath its empty seat were a large plastic bucket and an electric motor and gearbox connected to a pair of vertical rods. The whole thing was fitted with several sets of rubber straps, together with a pair of spiked mesh cups and sets of sharp crocodile clips that dangled menacingly.

'This is my Electrothrone,' Raven said proudly, as Angela shuddered in horror at the sight of it.

There was a table beside the chair with a control box on it, covered with old fashioned twist knobs, needle dials and switches. Lengths of electric flex connected it to the chair itself. Two cameras mounted on tripods were focused on the chair from different angles.

'Sit yourself down on it,' he told her.

What small measure of self-control she had built up deserted her. 'Please, no, don't make me... eeek!'

Raven jabbed her in the stomach with his cattle prod, making her double up in pain.

'What did I tell you about talking without permission? Now sit!'

Trembling and fearful, Angela clambered up onto the device and sat down. She had to spread her thighs wide so they were supported a little by the splayed sides of the empty seat. There was no front rail to the seat to hang her knees over, just a couple of large padded hooks. She had no choice but to place her knees into them, even though her cheeks burned at the way they forced her to expose herself. Still trying to support the weight of her upper body, her hands slid down the back legs of the chair past sets of dangling straps to a pair of handles, which she grasped hard.

Raven bound her to the device by pulling sets of straps about her thighs, knees and ankles, and wrists and elbows. A big strap went across her stomach. He removed her choke chain and another strap went across neck. He adjusted screw clamps that pressed rubber pads into sides of her head. He pushed a black rubber rod between her teeth, rather like a horses' bit.

'When the pain gets too much you can bite on that as much as you like,' he told her.

He pulled the spiked metal cups over her breasts like bra cups and strapped them into place. She yelped as the internal spikes pricked into her soft trembling globes, leaving only an open ring about her nipples. The dangling crocodile clips he fastened to her labia, making her yelp again as the sharp sprung teeth bit into her delicate flesh.

Then he pulled the wooden step aside and ducked down low between her splayed legs and adjusted the rods connected to the motor under the empty seat of the throne, sliding them up until the dildos on their ends pushed into the mouth of her vagina and the tight muscle ring of her anal sphincter. Angela sobbed as she felt the things being slid up into her, even as her nipples stood up hard.

Raven stood back and surveyed her with satisfaction. She was completely helpless and bound to the chair by so many straps she could hardly move. With the dildo rods half inside her, it was almost as if she was becoming part of it.

'There, you look lovely, as only an attractive, naked bound woman can be,' he declared. 'The idea is to reduce you to tears, until you beg to please me in any way I wish: after you have climaxed a few times to soften you up, of course. Now to make you sing...'

He turned to the control panel and began twisting knobs and throwing switches. Coloured lights flashed and things buzzed.

The dildos began to pump up inside her while alternating their thrusts, first plugging her vagina and then her rectum. She shuddered and moaned and dribbled about the gag bit. That was so primitive and intimate she could not help responding to it. She felt her nipples standing up hard, their swollen rims impaling themselves on spikes around them. Oh God was that sweat, or was she bleeding?

It wouldn't take much of this to make her cum, she thought dizzily. Then she shook her head. Climax in front of a masked man and his cameras while strapped to his torture chair? It would destroy her! But not Crystal. She could do this...

Then the spiked mesh domes over her breasts began to tingle with electricity, sending a thousand little shocks into her flesh. Angela's eyes bulged in pain and she screamed about her gag bit and then champed down hard on it. It felt as if her breasts had fire ants scrawling all over them. Her whole body began to jerk, straining on the straps that bound her to the chair frame.

Drool from her mouth dribbled off her chin onto the upper slopes of her imprisoned, spiked and zapped breasts.

Raven watched her intently, adjusting the dials and switches on its control panel. The twin dildos increased their pumping speed, probing deeper and deeper into her body. Then he pressed a new switch.

Angela screamed and almost bit through the gag bar, as the crocodile clips clamped about her labia came alive and drove intolerable jolts of hot and electric pain through her pussy. Her vagina clenched and she squeezed out a spurt of pee and dribbles of juices. The plunging dildos went wild inside her. She thought she would burst or burn. It was too much...

And then with a huge rush erupting from her loins, a massive orgasm enveloped her and she fainted clean away.

* * *

The next thing she knew, her bit gag been removed and Raven was feeding water from a squeeze bottle via a straw into her mouth. Clumsily she sucked it down. Her whole body ached and tingled and shuddered, but the dreadful electric current had been turned off and the dildos had been retracted.

'The bikers were right,' he said as she sucked on the straw, 'you really are rather special. I'm glad I bought you...'

And for a pathetic moment she actually felt a feeble thrill at this compliment.

'Now,' he continued, 'I'm going to put you through another session like the last one, but with everything turned up another notch in intensity... unless you have something else to suggest?'

'P... please... Sir... Mister Raven...' Angela rasped feebly. 'I'd love you to screw me right now... I beg you...'

And she felt the frightening pure thrill of total humiliating submission course through her.

Raven smiled and put down the water bottle and pushed her gag back into place.

He opened up his flies, freeing a large erection. He stepped between her splayed thighs, which she now realized were at just the right height for standing penetration. He unclipped the crocodile clips from her tingling, dripping labia and pushed the motor unit back a little to give him foot room. He wrapped his arms around her bound body. His chest pressed the spiked domes into her breasts, making her whimper, while her hard nipples were squashed up through the holes in their summits and were flattened against his black shirt.

His eyes, glittering under his mask, were level with hers. His cock found her wet gash and slid up into her. He began to pump into her.

And she felt her sheath clench shamelessly tight about him. She couldn't help it. That was the price of her surrender. The ice been broken and the secret hot slut underneath had been temporarily freed. She had been stimulated intolerably and now she needed release...

He thrust and she gasped and moaned and devoured him with her pussy.

Excited by her suffering, Raven did not need much more stimulation to climax. She felt his semen boil out of his cock tip and up into her vagina, which convulsed as it was filled and squirted its juices out over him.

And then she fainted again.

* * *

When Angela recovered, Raven had pulled out of her, leaving her dripping shamelessly.

For a few seconds she felt glorious. Everything was perfection. Then the ice began to form again.

'You really are a lovely screw, Crystal,' he said. 'If you weren't a hot potato, I'd keep you for months and have fun breaking you in every day. But I'll just have to do what I can in a few days...'

She groaned and snivelled and shook her head feebly.

'You want to say something?'

She nodded.

'You're not going to beg me to let you go, are you, because that would be a waste of time?'

She shook her head.

He pulled her gag bit out.

'Why…' She choked out. 'Why are you doing this? How can you be so cruel to me? What have I done to hurt you?'

Raven laughed. 'You have done nothing to justify this! You're totally innocent, which is part of your appeal. It's simply fun to see a pretty woman suffering. I belong to a secret circle of like-minded people, and that's what we do. We enjoy it. It's the most wonderful sport.' Then he wagged a finger. 'But we're responsible, enlightened and self-interested sadists. That's why we'll take good care of you and, at the proper time, we'll throw you back where you came from…'

* * *

Raven freed her from the Electrothrone. She was so weak she could hardly stand. She managed to look down her front, fearing the spikes on the insides of the metal cups had stabbed her breasts to ribbons, but there were only a few pricks and scratches and dribbles of blood. Because of the electric shocks passing through them as they had jabbed her, it had felt so much worse. He allowed her to wash again, using the enema tubes once more, and then she was fed and watered. Then he pushed her ball gag back in place.

'Now I'm going to put you in your cage for the night,' he told her.

It was shaped like a drum supported by a metal hoop that hung from a ceiling pulley. The ends of the hoop were pinned to swivel joints in the centres of each round face of the cage. She had to sit upright inside it, with her head protruding through a hole in the top and its sides pressing against her shoulders and hips and her legs bent and knees pulled up so they almost touched her breasts. Her buttocks rested against the lower curve of the cage bars. He pulled her arms round in front of her and through the upper bars of the cage and handcuffed them together outside it. He pulled her feet through gaps in the lower forward curve of the cage into projecting stirrups and cuffed them as well.

Raven paused for a moment to admire her totally helpless and confined body, and she stared back at him fearfully. 'That's how I want my slave to look at me,' he told her.

Angela felt her nipples hardening.

He worked the pulley to raise the cage off the ground. Mounted on its swivel joints it was free to tumble back or fourth around them, but as more of the mass of her body was below its centre of gravity than above, it remained upright. He lifted her until the cage was at waist height, then he locked the pulley off. He rotated the cage forward until her head was face down and her bottom was turned outwards, then he slid bolts in from the sides of the supporting hoop to engage with the cage rim, holding it in position.

He selected a lash from the array on the wall and ran his hands over her bottom flesh where it bulged out through the cage bars. Then he gave her bottom a good thrashing. Angela screamed and jerked frantically, but confined within the tight cage there was no escape.

It was not just her soft protruding posterior flesh that suffered. The pliant thongs curved in through the bars, snaking between them and smacking against her bottom cleavage and up between her thighs and against her pussy, even rasping into its cleft.

Angela sobbed and squirmed, making the cage swing from side to side. The pain was intense, and yet her exposure and confinement turned it into something else. Her pussy flushed and grew slippery and blossomed once again.

Only when she was a sobbing wreck did he pause to pull out her gag.

'Please... please... screw me, Sir,' she begged pitifully. It was so degrading to speak like that, but that moment she knew that she, or at least Crystal, needed that release.

'Where?' he asked.

Of course, he had her prepared her for this. 'Up my b… bum hole, Sir… Please…'

He pushed her gag back in again

Knowing what was expected of her she wriggled about, presenting her simmering buttocks cleft over a gap in the bars. He freed his cock and rammed it up into her tight anus. She squealed with pain and then clenched her bottom tight about him. He held onto the cage bars and drove his shaft deep into her again and again…

When he was finally done with her, and while her juices and his sperm dripped onto the rubber floor beneath, he went to the stairs and turned off the light and left her in the darkness to contemplate what she had just done and what more was to come.

Chapter Six

The next morning (at least she assumed it was morning and but without a clock or windows it was hard to tell) the lights came on again and Raven came down the stairs of the cellar dungeon.

After hours alone in the silent darkness, Angela was pathetically glad to see him as he lowered her cage and freed her from it. By then she was so cramped that she could hardly stand. He laughed and helped her to straighten out and then put her under the shower and washed and cleaned her. He fed her by hand with her kneeling in front of him. She knew what he was doing. He was making her feel totally dependent on him, as if he was training an animal to become obedient. But then she was totally dependent upon him.

He put her on the Electrothrone again. Now she knew what to expect, she trembled in fear of the things the device was going to do to her, even as she felt her nipples hardening and her pussy growing hot and slippery.

'Don't worry, Crystal, you won't be bored,' he promised her, as he buckled the spiked metal cups about her breasts, 'I've got something new to try out on you...'

He fitted a different head to the forward dildo rod. This one had a kind of saw-tooth rubber rasp curving up like a finger around the shaft of the dildo. He slid the shaft up into her and so that the rasp pressed into the cleft of her pussy. Then he went to the control panel and started the dildos pumping.

Her passageways were stretched and then sucked as the twin shafts alternated their thrusts. Her clamped labia sizzled and throbbed as shock after shock stabbed through them, while her spike-enclosed breasts throbbed and tingled and burned, gashing and pricking themselves with every jerk she made that set them bouncing with heavy fluid motion. She dribbled and drooled about the rubber bit clenched between her teeth; her spittle falling onto the heaving upper slopes of her breasts and running down under the spiked cups that encased them where it mingled with her fresh blood. But the rasp in her pussy was most wonderful and terrible difference.

It tore through her cleft, scraping her throbbing clitoris back and forth as if scrubbing it in a bath of sex juices. Even as she screamed and writhed in pain, the inescapable, incredible passion grew in her loins, filling her loins with hot liquid lust that then erupted in an outpouring of raw delight.

A stream of hot pee joined the eruption of her juices as she came, squirting messily around the rasp that was still embedded in her pussy cleft, and then she went limp.

Raven powered down the throne and squirted water from a squeezy bottle in her face to revive her. He pulled her gag bit out so he could feed her some of the water from bottle to help revive her. He kissed her stretched lips and then replaced the bit again. He pulled the dildos out of her pussy so he could get access to her groin, grinding himself against her sweaty body, and rammed his straining cock deep up into her sore wet throbbing pussy.

When he had taken his pleasure with her, while his sperm was still dripping out of her, he replaced the rasping dildo and started the throne up again…

* * *

After her third orgasm, Angela protested feebly. 'Please… Sir… I can't do this again… I can't take so much pain and pleasure the same time… it'll kill me…'

Of course it would not actually kill her, but she felt as if she would lose her mind to the power of the throne.

'Would you rather try another of my toys?'

'Yes… anything…'

'Maybe I'll try you on the Nevermore Machine…'

* * *

55

Angela lay doubled over so tightly on her back on the padded base board of the Nevermore Machine that she thought her back would break.

It did not break, of course, but it felt like it might. However, she could only make muffled hollow moans of pain and fear in response. She had a plastic funnel in her mouth taped to her lips with a clip on her nose that forced her to breathe through it. Raven was kneeling beside her pouring water into the funnel from a litre mineral water bottle which she had to gulp down quickly to keep breathing.

'You're almost ready,' he said, patting her doubled over belly which was now bulging from within.

She shook her head feebly and pleaded in between coughs and desperate gulps.

'Please… don't do this to me… master…screw me if you want to… just don't do this…'

'But you know I like to see you in distress. That's what slave girls are for…'

Her hips and bottom were raised by an angled wooden block pressed against her spine while a belt bolted to the back of the board and pulled tight over her stomach held her in place. Her arms were stretched downwards along her sides past the bracing block and secured to the lower end of the base board with screw clamps. Her legs were raised up and over her head and spread wide so that her knees rested next to her shoulders, where more clamps about their backs and her ankles held them in place. This enforced posture meant that every detail of her groin showing between her stretched thighs, with her anus pointing up at the ceiling exposed by the stretching of her buttock cleft, while the fleshy cleft of her pussy faced up the length of her body towards her head.

If this was not exposure enough, she had rubber garters straps bound about her upper thighs from which stretched elastic cords with hooks on their ends that were dug into her pussy lips pulling them open wide. Her inside passageways were totally exposed.

Then there were the bizarre fittings that gave the machine its name. There were two carved wooden black-painted ravens perched on the upper lip of the board bracing her back, so that their heads over her groin. Two more of the wooden birds stood on short rods on either side of her chest almost in her armpits so their heads overhung over her breasts. Their beaks were made of metal and needle sharp.

When Raven decided that Angela had drunk enough, he removed the funnel from mouth and unclipped her nose and pushed her ball gag back in. Then he went round to the little control panel and battery pack fitted to the back of its bracing block and threw a switch. Then he stood back to watch and enjoy her humiliation.

Hidden motors whirred and the wooden ravens began to bob and peck at her. At the same time, a recorded voice began to croak in a sinister tone: *Nevermore... nevermore...*

As they bobbed up and down jabbing her flesh with their sharp beaks, they slowly twisted from left to right and back again so that they attacked as much flesh as possible. They picked across her stretched buttocks and the cleft of her pussy. They swung about in arcs across her trembling breasts, passing over her hard nipples on the way. And as each beak jabbed into her, there was a little white electric flash as a current passed through it and flowed out through her body to complete the circuit via a metal plate pressing against her back.

Nevermore... nevermore...

Angela shrieked and sobbed and jerked at the relentless stabs of pain and needles of electric fire attacking the most sensitive parts of the body. The birds were pecking little bloody arcs in her flesh across her buttocks and the lips of her pussy and making strange speckled crimson crescents over her breasts.

And yet despite her tears and sobs, she felt herself responding with a slow perverse arousal. Her stretched and gaping pussy lips were swollen and she was dribbling juices down over the folds of her belly. Her nipples were hard and inflamed with blood, making them acutely sensitive each peck and stab of electricity.

Nevermore... nevermore...

Relentlessly the wooden birds attacked her: teasing and exciting and tormenting all the same time. It could only have one result...

With a sob Angela lost control of her own over-filled bladder and all the water she had been forced to drink spurted out of her cleft and down her body and over her face. She screwed up her eyes and spluttered and snivelled as the hot stream washed over her face and into her hair. For a full minute it continued to squirt, even as the birds eagerly pecked away at her wet pussy and soaked breasts, which now stung even more as the urine burned into her wounds.

Finally the stream subsided. Leaving her soiled and miserable and trembling in pain and yet also frighteningly aroused and desperate.

Raven folded down the wooden birds still attacking her groin so he could squat over it in reverse. He freed his hard cock and rammed it into her wet pussy and sat down on her taut buttocks as he filled her. And to her shame she clung and squeezed onto him until he filled her passage way with his seed and she came with a sob and a frantic shudder.

Nevermore... nevermore, the raven's croaked in mocking accompaniment.

After he was done, he got off her and took up the water bottle and plastic funnel and began to fill her up again...

* * *

58

That night, Raven put her in her circular cage again and lashed her and then he had her bottom. But this time he kept her tipped forward after he spent himself, and went round to her dangling head and removed her gag and pushed his now semi-hard penis between her lips. Wretchedly she sucked and licked the dregs of his sperm and the lubricating jelly he had used on her rear passage off his shaft.

As she did so, she realized that was the taste of her degradation.

Chapter Seven

The next morning, when Raven appeared, Angela could tell something had happened.

He explained as he petted her through her cage bars.

'I circulated your name and the vids I took of you to find out who might be interested in taking you off my hands for a good price. Unexpectedly I got a quick offer from somebody I know well, who goes by the name of Lady Syn, that I had to take up. I was planning to keep you for a few more days, but you are a hot potato and money talks...'

Angela gaped at him in horror. She had been sold on to another stranger and she was suddenly terrified. Tears overwhelmed her and for a minute she sobbed helplessly. Then she got a grip on herself again. Don't blub like a child! Use that cool intelligence she prized so much to survive this! Remember, this was happening to a woman called "Crystal". Angela Winston was not part of it.

Raven was stroking her. 'Better the devil you know, eh? Don't worry, Crystal. Lady Syn is very experienced. She'll take good care of you...'

Her self-control faltered and Angela sobbed again. How could she sustain such a piece of self-deception? And yet at this moment she did still feel detached and disbelieving, as if it was all happening to somebody else. Well let it!

Including those shocking, inexplicable orgasms? Yes, because that was how Crystal responded to rough handling. It was her little secret, her way of coping, even enjoying the experience.

But that was sick!

Yes, but it would fit right in with a dark world operating by different rules where nobody was who they said they were.

As a survival strategy she knew it was pitifully fragile, but it was all she had.

Raven took care to wash and clean her thoroughly, and fed her a decent breakfast. Then he produced the blackout hood again.

She whimpered and shook her head. 'Please don't use that on me again Sir… I beg you… it's frightening… I'll be good… I won't give you any trouble…'

Raven shook his head. 'Get used to it, Crystal. Everyone in the chain of people who'll have you will protect their true identities very carefully. The less you know about where you've been kept and what its like outside the quarters you are allowed to see the better. Then, when your safe time has expired, whoever has charge of you at that moment won't worry about throwing you back, knowing that if you do contact the police you won't be able to identify any of us. Now this stuff is safe when it's used properly. Just to breathe deeply…'

And he ignored her fear-filled eyes and pushed the ball gag back in place. Then doused the hood with the sleeping mixture and pulled it on over her head. After a few strained breaths, blackness engulfed her once again.

* * *

The next thing Angela saw was bright light streaming through skylight windows set in angled ceilings, looking as though they might have been the result of a loft conversion. After the gloom of Raven's cellar dungeon, the light stung her eyes. Still lightheaded from the sleeping drug, Angela rolled her eyes about, taking in her new surroundings.

The ceilings ran down to rows of fitted cupboards that ran down two sides of the big airy room. It had a polished board floor, scattered rugs, a pile of pillows in one corner and a large red comfy chair with a small dining table beside it. She was lying on her back on a

61

soft warm shag-pile rug. Her gag was still in place and her wrists were cuffed behind her back.

There were two figures standing over her and looking down on her. One was Raven and the other was a woman dressed in a red rubber cat-suit with a red cat half mask over her face. There were popper-closed panels over her breasts and crotch. As Angela awoke, she was prodding her with her bare toes that protruded from the tips of her red sling-back sandals.

'Yes, she does look very pretty,' she was saying. 'But is she really a hot potato?'

'She should be safe until the twenty-fourth,' Raven said. 'Then you'll have to dispose of her.'

'You're asking a lot of money for a short-term leash.'

'She's worth it. And if you advertise her properly, then you'll make it back.'

'Is she really as passionate as she appeared in the videos?'

'Once you break down her resistance it pours out of her,' Raven assured her. 'She seems to bottle it up until it has to escape. Then she can't control herself. When she's on a high, she can't get enough cock and she drinks up pain until she's exhausted. When she recovers, I think she's ashamed of herself. She's denying her true nature. Clearly she's a natural submissive but won't admit it. I guarantee you'll have fun with her...'

'I'm sure I will,' said Lady Syn.

An envelope changed hands. Raven bent down and removed the choke chain from Angela's neck. 'Don't fight what you are inside, Crystal,' he said, giving her breasts one last squeeze. Then he left.

Crystal had been sold once again.

* * *

Lady Syn knelt down and buckled a fresh collar about Angela's neck. It was deep red rubber and was fastened

62

to a red leather leash. Then she rolled her over onto her front and pulled soft red rubber mittens over Angela's hands. They were fingerless and thumbless, reducing her hands outwardly to something more like paws.

Lady Syn patted and stroked Angela's bare bottom. 'Yes, I think I'm going to have a lot of fun with you,' she said half to herself.

She pulled on the leash and Angela squirmed and rolled herself onto her knees. She was dragged across the floor to the big chair where the end of the leash was hooked over one arm. Lady Syn seated herself comfortably in the chair. Angela knelt with her legs submissively apart as Raven had taught her, facing her new owner feeling sick and terrified and a little bit excited.

Lady Syn's bright green eyes flashed behind her mask and Angela in turn looked around her up and down. Taking in what she could see of her face Angela realized that she was a middle-aged woman, perhaps fifteen years older than her, with a good if slightly fleshy figure. Then she bent forward and pulled out Angela's gag.

'Are you going to be my good little kitten, Crystal?' she asked.

Angela licked her dry lips. Was there any point in defying her? 'Yes… Mistress, I will be your good little kitten,' she promised. She felt a dark thrill at her own submissive words, which made her heart sink. No, she couldn't submit as easy as that. 'But I'd rather be free, Mistress,' she added.

'So, Raven was right. You are a feisty one.'

'I'm just a normal woman who knows right from wrong, Mistress,' Angela insisted.

'We'll see about that,' Lady Syn said with a smile. 'Now, will you squeal and mew when I hurt you and cum when I make you, or do I have to beat that admission out of you as well?'

63

Angela shuddered. She meant it. This was where her defiance ended for the moment. 'No, Mistress... I mean... yes... I'll do all that... but I won't like it.'

Lady Syn rubbed her fingers through the tight rubber of her groin which moulded itself to the contours of her barely concealed her pubic cleft.

'Will you use your pretty pink tongue to pleasure me when I command you?'

Angela gulped. She had never made love to woman before. 'Yes, Mistress, I will use my tongue to p... pleasure you.'

Lady Syn patted Angela on the head. 'Good kitten.'

The table beside the chair was set out with a glass carafe of orange juice and a glass and a red enamelled bowl. Lady Syn poured juice out into both of them and sipped from the glass. Then she put the bowl down in front of Angela.

'Now I want to see you drink like a kitten. Lap it up...'

Awkwardly, Angela hunkered down, spreading her legs wider and dipping her back and sticking out her bottom to maintain her balance so that she could lower her head over the bowl. Her hot breasts and hard nipples brushed against the polished floor.

She sucked and lapped at the orange juice as well as she could, making an unavoidable mess. Apparently was easier if you had a snout and a long tongue.

But Lady Syn seemed pleased with her efforts and patted her head again. 'Good kitten,' she said, 'keep on drinking...'

While she was lapping away, Lady Syn got up and went over to one of the cupboards and brought out a low squat square post on wheels that she positioned in the middle of the room. There were a lot of straps and chains and hooks dangling from it. A second wheeled rack followed it. Angela rolled her eyes up from her bowl to see it held an array of punishment straps, paddles, dildos, canes, tawses and lashes, all of red leather or rubber or red painted.

Angela shivered in fear. Her new mistress was just as much of a sadist as Raven, only more brightly coloured.

When Angela had lapped up all of the orange juice she could manage, Lady Syn replaced her ball gag and unhooked her leash from the chair and led her, still shuffling on her knees, over to the post. She jerked on the leash so that she stood up far enough to sit on the padded top of the post with her bottom projecting over one side. She pulled a strap over the tops of Angela's thighs, holding her in place. Then she lifted up her legs and strapped them to the base of the post on either side of it. There was a telescopic rod resting vertically against the face of the post between Angela's legs which was hinged at the bottom. Lady Syn removed Angela's leash and unfolded the rod outwards and extended it so that its end clipped to the front of her collar, bracing her neck and holding her head up, forcing her to look straight ahead. She selected a short sprung chain from the rack of implements and connected one end into a ring on the back of Angela's collar and the other to her cuffed wrists, pulling them up her back.

Now Angela was bent over the top of the post with her haunches and groin and buttocks totally exposed. She would have toppled over forward but for the straps holding her thighs down and the bracing of the telescopic rod under her chin. This presented both her head and breasts and buttock cleft and pussy for Lady Syn's inspection.

She knelt in front of her to examine her face closely, cupping and squeezing her dangling breasts as she did so. Then she kissed her lips stretched by the gag ball between her teeth, shocking Angela with the sense of her passion. Smiling, Lady Syn un-popped the panels of her rubber cat-suit that concealed her own breasts and let them hang out freely. They were plump pink mounds with hard dark nipples.

Lady Syn held Angela's head by her hair and rubbed her face into her cleavage, squashing her breasts against her nose and mouth.

Then she stood up and opened the panel of the cat suit over her groin, exposing her plump pink hairless vulva. Taking hold of Angela's hair again, she ground her face into her pussy cleft. Angela smelt perfume and the intimate female scent of her arousal.

'Soon I'll have you licking me out properly, Crystal,' she promised. 'But first you need to be warmed up...'

She moved round to kneel behind Angela and peered up into her groin, stroking her flesh. She pried open the cleft of her buttocks to examine her anus, and then rubbed her stiff fingers through the gash of her pussy. Helplessly, Angela shivered with pleasure at her touch. It was her only escape from what was to come. She must let Crystal take over...

'Yes, very pliant and moist and lush...' Lady Syn said, 'but I think it could be hotter...'

She selected a red leather lash from the array and stroked it across Angela's jutting posterior. And then she raised her arm and brought the lash down hard.

It swished and cracked, curling its thongs lasciviously about her soft flesh, and Angela screamed about her gag, feeling hot tears filling her eyes.

Again and again the lash fell, curving up into her most intimate places, tearing through her cleft and smacking into her clitoris. Angela twisted and squirmed and jerked frantically as the waves of pain coursed through her. Her dangling breasts bobbed and swayed and grew hot with excitement that foretold the beginnings of perverse arousal. She let it flow through her.

Lady Syn paused her beating to feel Angela's groin and her fingers came away wet and sticky. 'That's better,' she said. She rubbed the thongs of the lash through Angela's dripping cleft, soaking in her juices, and then rubbed them through her own naked pussy. 'Oh yes, you really are lovely and wet…'

She moved round to Angela's head and rubbed the wet thongs into her face. She inhaled the scent her own excitement and felt dizzy. Then Lady Syn swung the lash up under Angela's jutting body so they cracked against her dangling breasts, making them shiver and jump. Fresh tears filled Angela's eyes.

When Angela's breasts were simmering pink melons, Lady Syn hung the lash back on the rack and selected a large red strap on dildo. She plugged its rubber prong-lined groin pad and smaller shaft up into herself and strapped it about her waist and then took hold of Angela's hips and rammed the rubber jelly shaft up into her dripping pussy with vicious passion. And as it filled her again and again, making her vulva bulge, Crystal thought: yes, I want more of this!

And then everything exploded.

* * *

Half an hour later, Angela was in Lady Syn's bathroom but she could see none of it.

After her post screwing, she had been blindfolded with opaque swimming goggles and then taken downstairs to a landing and then the bathroom. She reminded herself that for a hot potato like her, blindfolds were good and ignorance was bliss. But of course, it also made her even more helpless, so that her mistress had even more power over as she handled her and moved her about.

She was sat on a bidet so that her groin and burning bottom could be flushed clean. Then she was put under a shower, with her leash hung over some hook above her head. Lady Syn removed her cat-suit and then joined her

67

in the shower totally naked. She meticulously soaked Angela all over and then rubbed her own naked body against hers. She used a short-handled back-scrubbing brush to tease her nipples and clitoris, and then she smacked it against Angela's bare wet bottom. Her fingers explored the clefts of her buttocks and pussy and worked their way deep up into them.

The handle of the brush was turned around and pushed up into Angela's vagina until its head alone jutted out between her thighs, making her gasp. Lady Syn pushed her into a corner of the shower cubicle and kissed her passionately, all the while grinding her own pussy against the bristles of the brush jutting out between Angela's thighs.

'You are going to be so good,' she promised her.

She felt herself flushed with helpless desire and dizzy and confused by this masterful females' domination. It was right that she was touched and used, Crystal thought.

When she was dry, she was taken back upstairs to the loft playroom. Her leash was fastened to some hook high on one wall.

'I'm just going to prepare some food,' Lady Syn said, stroking her bare breasts. 'We're going to dine together...'

Angela was left to stand there, naked, collared, cuffed and blindfolded, while Lady Syn went downstairs again.

After a few minutes, Angela found herself squirming awkwardly. She was not in any pain or actual discomfort at that moment, but just being left like an animal to wait for the return of her mistress was an ordeal its own right. Without any effort on Lady Syn's part, it made her appreciate the degree of her own helplessness. How long before she would begin wishing for the return of her mistress? Fear began to grow inside her. Had she forgotten about her? She could be left here for hours or days…

It could only have been half an hour before Lady Syn returned. By that time Angela had got so anxious that she felt a swell of relief inside her as she entered the loft room.

'Now we're going to eat,' Lady Syn said, removing Angela's blindfold.

There was a meal on a tray on the table beside the big chair. But there was only one set of cutlery.

Angela was made to kneel on the floor beside Lady Syn's chair eating chopped food out of a bowl like a dog or cat would. As Lady Syn sat at a table eating her own meal, occasionally she stroked Angela's naked body with her bare feet. A few times she fed her morsels of food on the end of her own fork and Angela had to take it from her. And the terrible thing was, that felt right and exciting.

The dessert was a mixed fruit salad with cream. But this time there was no bowl for Angela. Lady Syn turned her chair round to face Angela. She opened the groin flap of her cat suit, took up a grape dripping with cream and pushed it up into her plump pussy.

'Eat,' she told Angela.

With a shiver, Angela pressed her face into her groin and sought the bit of food with her tongue. Lady Syn shivered and patted her head as her face ground against her pussy.

When Angela eventually retrieved the grape, she swallowed it down. Lady Syn smiled and took a cube of chopped pineapple and pushed it a little deeper into her pussy.

'Eat,' she told her again.

Angela dipped her head again…

As she retrieved the tenth piece of fruit from Lady Syn's pussy, she gave a little moan and shudder and came over Angela's face.

69

'Oh… Yes… Good girl,' she said, patting her head.

* * *

When the light faded in the skylight windows, Lady Syn blindfolded Angela again and then took her downstairs.

After a quick visit to the bathroom to freshen up, she was led into another room and made to clamber up onto something yielding. It felt like the end of a bed. Then she was pressed against some kind of vertical lattice frame of tubular metal rods. Her legs were spread and strapped to the frame by ankles, thighs and waist. Her cuffed her arms were freed and stretched upwards and her wrists were secured to the upper corners of the frame. Only then were her blindfold goggles removed.

She was standing inside a modern four-poster bed. Its curtains had been pulled across, so she had no idea what lay outside it. That was good, she reminded herself.

Lady Syn was naked again, except for her cat mask, smiling and stroking her. Then she bent down and extended some kind of rod from the base of the frame up into Angela's rectum. It had a complicated twin pronged head. One plug went into her rectum while the other hinged up forward and a bulbous plug on its inner side was pushed up into her vagina. This left a jutting external red rubber phallus standing out from between her thighs.

Lady Syn lay down on the bed with her legs wide and touched a control button on the side of his head board.

The frame began to tilt forward, carrying Angela with it. She was lowered down over Lady Syn's body, who shifted her hips so that the phallus slid up into her. Now they were face-to-face and breast to breast. Lady Syn pressed another button and the rod lodged in Angela's rear began to pump up and down and vibrate.

Angela shuddered as the dildo plugs pulsated within her. The vibrations were also transmitted by the phallus

70

into Lady Syn's pussy. She was being compelled to screw her!

She saw her smiling happily under her cat mask as she squirmed underneath her, rubbing her breasts together and lifting her hips to grind against Angela's. She had been turned into a fleshy vibrating dildo for her pleasure. It was totally shameful and degrading... and incredible!

The smell of the older woman's excitement filled her nostrils and suddenly Angela found herself kissing her with her gagged lips and her passion was returned redoubled.

And then she came explosively even as Lady Syn bucked underneath her. And for a few seconds everything was perfect.

* * *

The next day in the loft playroom, Lady Syn used rubber straps to bind Angela's lower legs, which were bent sharply at the knees against the backs of her thighs, so that her heels pressed against her buttocks. Then she fitted rubber paw pads to her knees to go with the ones enclosing her hands.

Treating her like a dog again, Lady Syn sat in her big chair and she threw rubber balls and rubber bones about the room and Angela had to run about on her hands and, literally, knees, and fetch them in her mouth and return them neatly to her mistress's hand and receive a pat on the head as a reward. And it was perverse mad fun, and her breasts bounced merrily and her nipples throbbed with hardness and excitement.

After a while, Lady Syn began dipping the ends of the rubber bones into her own pussy juices and then throwing them, Angela had retrieved them while they dripped with her juices. Then she dipped them into Angela's pussy and she had to taste her own excitement as she picked them up in her mouth.

71

'I wish I could take you for a walk in the park just like this,' Lady Syn said, stroking her.

To make her task a little more challenging, she fastened a rubber football on the end of a chain with bulldog clips to the lips of Angela's pussy and she had to pull that after her as she ran up and down. The ball jerked and bobbed and bounced between her knees, yanking on her soft pussy lips. She sobbed and yelped even as she fetched and ran. She realized how painful and demeaning it was. How could she get carried away and allow herself to enjoy being treated like this?

It's easy, said Crystal.

And then suddenly she came and collapsed on the floor.

* * *

That night Lady Syn lay on top of Angela's back in the bed while she was strapped face down and spread wide. Angela sobbed and bit on the rubber bit in her mouth as Lady Syn rammed a succession of ever larger dildos up into her bottom. She thought she would burst, but she didn't. It only made the orgasms when they came even more intense.

After they had come for the third time, Lady Syn lay sweaty and satisfied on her back with her hands beneath her, squeezing Angela's breasts idly. I can survive this with Crystal's help, Angela thought. And when it's all over, she will disappear and I'll return and it will be as if it never happened...

And then Lady Syn spoke huskily in her ear. 'You've been a lovely hot potato to play with, Crystal, but I've already had a good offer for you. Tomorrow I'm passing you on to somebody who'll also appreciate your special qualities...'

Angela felt a sudden surge of fear and anger at the idea that she had been sold on some new dominator without being consulted. And then this resentment was confused by a sharp pang of dismay at the thought of leaving her mistress. No, that was all wrong! Oh God, she was getting so screwed up!

Chapter Eight

He called himself "The Headmaster."

He was a tall lean man, perhaps in his mid-fifties, who wore an old-fashioned mortarboard and black academic robes and shiny black shoes and black socks, but with no trousers. His heavy penis and scrotum, covered in greying pubic curls, dangled between lean thighs. His face was disguised behind a pair of fake tinted glasses with a fake plastic nose and moustache attached. It would have been comic in other circumstances, but Angela did not laugh.

Angela, while she was still dizzy from the after effects of the knockout hood, had been put into a costume to compliment his. She now wore a white shirt with its front unbuttoned to expose her cleavage, a school tie, no bra, and a short pleated grey skirt with no knickers, white ankle socks and black shoes. Her hair had been tied up in bunches. She was the very image of a slutty fantasy schoolgirl.

They were in a large room that had been carefully fitted and decorated to look like an old-fashioned schoolroom.

There were maps and pictures of famous places, people and things pinned to the walls. The high windows were filled with pebble glass so there was no view out or in. A single student's desk and chair faced an old-fashioned high teachers chair and desk. There was a rack of canes on the wall beside it. There was an old-fashioned blackboard mounted on a wooden A-frame. The back half of the classroom became a kind of gymnasium. There was a set of wall bars and a pair of thick climbing ropes hung from the ceiling. A vaulting box rested in stacked layers in one corner, while rubber gym mats lay on the floor.

The place smelt of chalk dust and polish.

But Angela has had little time to take in all this. She was being inspected…

She stood before the Headmaster with her skirt lifted up in front of her, so that he could rub his fingers over her pussy. Her shaven hair was starting to grow back...

'Bristles!' he said in disgust. 'You're growing pubic hair, Crystal? Don't you know that's against school rules?'

'No, Headmaster I'm sorry, Headmaster,' Angela said meekly, trembling with fear.

'That's no excuse. Six of the best! Bend over and hold onto your ankles…'

She bent over, grasping her ankles. He lifted her skirt to expose her bottom. He selected a cane and thwacked it across her backside half a dozen times, pausing between each blow to feel how much heat he was beating into her flesh and fingering her pouting cleft, which grew hotter and wetter with each blow. She yelped and squirmed but she did not attempt to escape her absurd punishment. There was no escape. The only door out of the room was securely locked and the Headmaster had the only key. She had to play out this fantasy by his rules…

By the time he was done, her eyes were red with tears and his cock was straining hard.

'Now let's get rid of those bristles!' he declared.

She lay on his high sloping desk with her legs spread wide and her crotch facing him. Her hot buttocks overhung the lower edge of the desk. He pushed her hands back down on either side of her head and concealed spring clamps snapped out of the top of the desk and closed about her wrists.

'Do you want to conform to school rules, or do you want another caning, girl?' he asked sternly.

'Yes, Sir… I mean no Sir… I mean, please Sir, will you shave me, Sir…' she begged.

She lay there while he lovingly applied soap to her pussy with an old-fashioned bristle shaving bush and then carefully shaved her clean and smooth once more. When he was done, he wiped her dry with a tissue.

He rubbed his fingers through her now perfectly hairless cleft. 'That's more like it,' he declared.

Then he stood up and took hold of her splayed thighs and rammed his hard cock up into her. She gasped and arched her back as he filled her to the hilt. The old desk creaked and groaned under the weight of his pounding. She was aware of his eyes shining down at her through his fake glasses, watching the heave and sway of her breasts moving under her white school shirt, playing peek-a-boo with its open front. This was sick so she let Crystal enjoy it. It was getting easier each time to let go...

She felt him spout his sperm up inside her and felt an orgasmic shudder of her own in response

After savouring his mastery over her for several moments, he pulled out of her and wiped his cock clean on her inner thighs. Then he pressed some hidden button and the spring clamps freed her wrists.

'Now go back to your desk, you naughty girl, and get back to work...'

* * *

Work consisted of copying some long complex essay written in Latin from a printed chart he had hung over the blackboard. While she worked, the headmaster prowled about the room, peering over her shoulder and down her cleavage. Every so often he slipped his hand in under her shirt and cupped and squeezed her hot breasts. She had to hold still and let him fondle her while still trying to work.

Inevitably, this distracted her and she made a mistake in her copying. He snatched up her exercise book and jabbed his finger at an error.

'You stupid girl! Wrong, wrong, wrong... into the corner with you...'

She had to stand in the corner of the room next the blackboard facing inwards with a big white Dunces cap on her head and with her skirt rolled up and legs apart and hands braced against the wall. He used a long whippy cane to beat her bottom. It was far worse in her first caning. Every stroke seared into her, making her bottom flesh rippled while she shrieked and jerked. After a dozen strokes of the cane, the pain got the better of her self control and she peed onto the floor.

'Filthy girl!' he shouted.

That got her another dozen strokes.

By the time he was finished, she was trembling and sobbing and her bottom was raw and she was standing in a pool of her own pee.

He left there for an hour. Then he gave a bucket and mop and she had to clean up her own mess. Then she was allowed to go back to the desk and sit down gingerly onto her blazing bottom.

* * *

When it came time to eat lunch, she had to crawl on her hands and knees up to his desk and take bites out of sandwiches that he held out for her. When she was fed, she had to thank him.

'Thank you, Headmaster, for giving me my meal,' she said meekly.

'Don't you want to drink as well, Crystal?' he asked, swinging round in his chair and parting his legs suggestively.

Trying not to choke, she shuffled forward and took his cock in her mouth and bobbed her head and sucked on it until he came down her throat. She swallowed it down and then she had to thank him again.

'Thank you for that drink of your sperm, Headmaster,' she said huskily.

77

And then she shuffled off back to her desk. She was horribly aware that her pussy dripped on the way.

* * *

The light in the pebbled windows was dimming. Presumably school was over for the day, Angela thought. What would happen now?

Headmaster pressed a button and an electric bell rang. 'Class is dismissed, except for Crystal,' he said. 'In view of your slovenly behaviour and poor work, you will remain behind serving a detention. Come up here... take your shirt and tie and skirt off...'

Angela spent the night alone in the darkened make-believe schoolroom tied to the A-frame that normally supported the blackboard, with the Headmaster's sperm dribbling out of her sore pussy. She was gagged by her own school tie. Her arms had been pulled up over her head and strapped with her wrists crossed to the apex of the frame, while her legs were spread wide and strapped at the knees and ankles to its splayed forward facing struts. A bucket to catch her pee rested between her legs.

The wooden pegs that went into the holes in the frame that supported the board at different heights had been put to fresh uses. One had been pushed up into her vagina and the other her rectum. Their hard phallic shapes seemed to grind together inside her. She had been warned what would happen to her if they were not still inside her when the Headmaster opened up the classroom the next morning.

The peg in her bottom seemed secure enough, held in place by her anal sphincter, but she feared the one in her vagina might slip out. The trouble was that the tighter she clenched about it, the wetter and more slippery it became. She did not want another punishment. There were half a dozen red stripes across her chest, curving around the slopes of her breasts, where he had caned them both for her poor performance today, and as a warning to try harder tomorrow.

* * *

The next day, the Headmaster gave Angela a gym class.

For this, she had a change of uniform. She had to wear a tight white T-shirt top that showed every detail of her breasts and nipples, and an equally tight pair of navy blue knickers, which cut into the cleft of her shaven pussy, together with white socks and plimsolls.

While the Headmaster stood in the middle of the gym floor holding a long-shafted cane, Angela had to run around a continuous loop of the equipment. She had to vault the box, climb up one end of the wall bars and shuffle along the top rungs and descend the other, clamber up one of the climbing ropes and then swing across and slide down the other one, and then perform cartwheels along a row of mats back to the box once more.

Soon she was sweating profusely, which only made her skimpy garments cling to her even more revealingly. She could feel the headmaster's eyes on her jiggling breasts and sweaty crotch as she circled about him. What schoolgirl fantasies was he playing out his mind? Pervert, she thought, in disgust.

And yet try she might, she, or at least Crystal, could not help but become aroused by her own performance. Her nipples were standing up hard through the top, while her pussy was growing wet and making a stain on her knickers. She was acutely aware of him staring at that stain every time she performed her cartwheel on the mats in front of him. Which of course only made her pussy even wetter…

Climbing the ropes was the hardest part, even though they had been knotted at regular intervals to help her keep a grip. She had to wind her legs around them as the ropes slid up or down through her crotch. Every knot had to pass between her sweaty thighs, scraping over her wet snickers, digging into the furrow of her sex and teasing her clit. By the time she descended the second rope, she was squirming with shameful arousal.

After several circuits she began to tire, which meant the Headmaster used his cane more often. It swished and cracked across her sweaty thighs, hot buttocks and barely confined breasts, beating down her hard nipples. As her final cartwheels got more ragged, he began to swipe it down into her crotch as she splayed her legs. This caused her to sprawl as she tumbled with a yelp of pain. Immediately the cane was swiped over her shivering body, driving her on again.

'No stamina, Crystal?' The Headmaster snapped angrily, flicking and jabbing at her with his cane. 'You're just the same pathetic, slutty, lazy girl you always were. On your feet! Another circuit... get on with it!'

Finally, her legs gave way and Angela collapsed in a sweaty heap face down on the mats panting and gasping. She could not run another step, far less climb anymore ropes or wall bars.

'So, you've given up, you miserable wretch!' The Headmaster said. 'You're going to have to be punished for that, Crystal. Get those clothes off!'

Feebly, hardly able to move her aching limbs, she stripped off her sodden shirt and knickers.

He picked up her sweaty knickers and rolled them up into a ball and forced them into her mouth. She could taste her own sweat and excitement. Then he grabbed her by the hair and dragged her over to the vaulting box. He heaved her over its padded top so that her head overhung one side and her legs the other. Then he uncoiled ropes that had been tied to many rings screwed to its sides and bound around her wrists and ankles, spreading her wide.

He rubbed his hands over her hot naked sweaty bottom and felt her dripping groin.

'You have been taking carnal pleasure from your exercise. That is not allowed by the school rules!'

He selected something else from the punishment rack. It was an old-fashioned wooden yard-long ruler, marked out only in inches.

He took up position behind Angela and stroked it across her bottom. She shuddered. Then he raised his arm and swung!

The crisp smack the yard rule made was startling, echoing about the room. A broad stripe of her bottom flesh was beaten inwards, sending ripples out on either side of it. Angela screamed through her knicker-gag as tears filled her eyes. The Headmaster raised the yard rule again...

A dozen times he beat her bottom, carefully spreading out each blow across the twin hemispheres until they were one uniform scarlet to glow of hot flesh. By that time Angela was howling and sobbing with pain and was hardly thinking straight. She had been such a bad girl... she deserved this...

The Headmaster felt her blazing bottom and then pushed the tip of the terrible yard rule up between her thighs and sawed it through her wet cleft, jabbing her clitoris. She shuddered and groaned and squirmed with sudden arousal.

'A slut to the end, eh, Crystal?' he said with contempt.

He dropped the ruler and rammed his straining cock up into her pussy, reaching across the top of the vaulting box to brace himself, shoving his shaft into her again and again like a frenzied machine until he spurted inside her. As if that was the trigger she had been waiting for, Angela felt another titanic orgasm tear through her. And then there was only welcoming blackness.

* * *

Angela had no idea how long she slept, recovering from exhaustion, the caning and screwing. All she knew was

81

that the light was dimming in the school windows when she opened her crusted eyes again.

The headmaster lifted her head up by her hair gave her a glass of water to drink.

'Your lessons are over, Crystal,' he told her. 'You have been a perfect slutty pupil. Tomorrow, you're going to another private institution, where I have suggested that they are even stricter with you...'

Chapter Nine

They called themselves "Jack" and "Jill", and they were a middle-aged couple who wore smiling boy and girl facemasks with rosy cheeks painted on them. Angela imagined their real faces were as delighted as their masks made them seem the morning they first set eyes upon her, after undoing her from the sack in which she had been delivered to them.

'Oh, isn't she lovely, Jack?' Jill said. 'What lovely titties…' she squeezed and pinched them. 'And lovely hard nipples…'

'And a nicely shaven pussy,' Jack said. 'I do like that. So clean and hygienic…'

They kept Angela in what closely resembled an old-fashioned bed and playroom, except that its primary coloured double bed had straps and chains hung from it with mirrors on the ceiling above, there was a big brightly painted cupboard filled with every kind of restraint and punishment devices and its windows were barred and the glass was covered by adhesive sheets of misty translucent plastic. The adjacent en suite bathroom had hooks screwed into its walls and a restraining frame mounted over its bidet.

It was while she was fastened to this that they flushed her out with enema tubes and washed her over until she met their standards of cleanliness and hygiene. To keep her vulva perfectly smooth, Jill applied depilating cream to it.

While it did its work, Jill made Angela up, painting red spots on her cheeks and applying bright red lipstick to her lips. She applied a heavy layer of blue highlighter around her eyes and then combed her hair back and platted it into a pigtail. Finally, she painted all of Angela's nails white.

Then Jack did a bizarre thing: he applied superglue to the insides of Angela's fingers and stuck them together forming single flaps of flesh. Only then did Angela realize what they were doing: they were making a living doll of her.

'No speaking, Crystal,' they warned her. 'It's a rule of our house. Little squeaks and squeals are permitted, and of course tears, but never a word, do you understand?'

Fearfully she nodded.

When she was ready, they cuffed her wrists behind her back and took her to the bed.

Apart from its bright colours, it seemed to be a modern bed with large heavy square posts at its corners. Then Jack pulled on the cap on one of them and a concealed post extended up out of it, carrying a section of the foot rail of the bed with it, looking a little like a gibbet arm. When it was fully extended, it reached well above head height. He swung its end out over the floor at the foot of the bed. The gibbet arm had a hook on its end. From the big cupboard, Jack took out a length of thick rope with one end formed into a noose with a ring on the other that he hung onto the end of the gibbet.

By this time, Angela was trembling in fear and dreadful anticipation. But she knew by now that there was no point in protesting, even if she had not been told to keep quiet. These were clearly experienced slave handlers and would do whatever they wanted to her and there was nothing she could do about it.

Sure enough they put the noose over her head and adjusted shortened the rope until she had to stand directly under it on tiptoe. She found the rope was too thick to cut into her neck and was too loose to choke her: as long as she remained still.

Jack and Jill stripped off, except for their masks, revealing greying but still quite well toned bodies.

They took out new items from the big cupboard: a pair of brightly coloured spanking paddles.

'We like to give all our new toys a good paddling as soon as we get them, so we know they'll be properly obedient,' Jill explained, swishing her paddle through the air vigorously.

'Open up,' said Jack, pushing something into Angela's mouth.

It was kind of gag she had not yet seen. It was of rubber with springs inside it which went between her teeth and clamped about her tongue. It had a protruding bar across its end by which it could be positioned and removed: squeezing on it opened and closed its clamp end. This bar was curved and moulded in red rubber to resemble a pair of smiling lips.

Jack and Jill took up position on either side of her and swung their paddles.

Angela screamed through her strange gag which muffled her cry of pain.

Enthusiastically, Jack and Jill beat her from neck to knees, not sparing her breasts or bottom or groin, their paddles swishing through the air and smacking into her flesh, leaving stinging red blotches behind them. They did not cut her skin but they delivered sharp stinging stabs of pain that soon had Angela sobbing and squirming frantically.

Tears dribbled out of her brightly highlighted eyes over her made up cheeks and down onto her heaving, trembling, shivering breasts. Dribble ran out of the corners of her smiling plastic lips and joined them.

As the couple beat her, she saw through her tears that Jack's cock had stiffened into a hard rod, while Jill's crimson nipples were standing up hard. Her suffering was giving them so much pleasure...

They only desisted when she was swaying drunkenly with the pain, the noose rasping about her neck. By then her body was glowing shocking pink and stinging all over.

They unhooked the noose from the gibbet arm and used it to drag her up onto the bed, spreading her legs wide. Getting four more shorter and thinner rope nooses with hooked ends from the cupboard they hung them around the posts of the bed and then tighten them around her outstretched ankles. Then they unclipped her arms from behind her back and stretched them out to the top end of the bed and secured them in turn.

Jack squirmed and slid himself under Angela's spread-eagled body, reaching round to cup and squeeze her breasts, until his hard cock slid up into her rectum. Jill had gone to the cupboard again and taken out a big pink double ended dildo. She plugged one in into herself and then mounted Angela.

The big pink dildo slid up inside her, parting her pussy lips wide and filling her vagina. Jill's breasts flattened against hers. Angela looked up into her smiling plastic face. How could she do this to another woman while her husband had his cock up her arse, she wondered?

And then the pair began to grind her between them; impaling her on a rod of flesh up her rear passageway and a shaft of soft plastic in her front one. Her freshly beaten flesh tingled as their skin pressed against hers. Angela thought the two shafts would split her open or meet inside her. She jerked and squirmed and cried, which seemed to encourage her new master and mistress, who pumped even harder into her.

And all the time she gasped and sobbed, her plastic lips kept smiling.

* * *

There was a big dolls house mounted against one wall of the playroom, the front of which opened into two panels revealing a slave cage behind it. It was in here that Angela was confined after they had finished their first session with her. It had a well-padded floor that she could lie down on in some comfort. They closed both the inner cage door and the front panels of the dolls house, leaving her only able to see out through its tiny windows. It was double security as she heard Jack and Jill carefully lock the door of the playroom from the outside when they went out.

She was left alone for a few hours. The house, if that was what it was, seemed totally silent. Had Jack and Jill gone out? Well they must have some other interests in life apart from playing with their new living doll, she conceded. She imagined it was something incredibly respectable so that their friends would never guess their secret vice. This house could be situated in some gentile suburban street that she would never see and name she would never know.

Resting also gave her time to assess her feelings as rationally as she could in the circumstances. She, or rather Crystal, was bearing up reasonably well, she decided. She was surviving, just about, by enduring her ordeal from day to day. The days were important. She had been keeping track of the date. This was the eleventh. She was over a third of the way through her sexual odyssey. What she would feel like at the end, she could only guess.

But would it end in freedom as promised? If she had a chance to escape, she must take it…

She must have dozed because she was jerked awake by the front of the dolls' house being opened. Jack and Jill pulled her out of her cage and took her back to bed for another session of smacking and screwing.

* * *

The next day, Jack and Jill took some time preparing Angela for a special event.

'There's a master and slave party tonight that we're going to take you to,' Jack said. 'It's always nice to be to show off new toys to your friends…'

Angela was put into a black rubber corset, which clung to her hips and curved up under her breasts

87

without covering them, and a tight black rubber hood and face mask that covered her head and neck down to her collarbones and moulded itself to her skin. The only openings in it were zip flaps over her eyes and mouth and a hole over her nostrils. It had a slot at the back where her newly plaited hair could hang through.

Her red lipped tongue clamp was replaced by a black one to go with her new costume. It meant that even when her mouth was unzipped, she would not be able to speak.

Over her hood went a rubber collar with a trailing chain leash. Fifteen centimetre black high heels were slid onto her feet which locked about her ankles. An adjustable hobble chain linked them together. Her glued hands were held down to her sides by black cuffs which were linked by short chains to black rubber garters.

By contrast, Jack and Jill dressed up in respectable smart party clothes, with the addition of their usual smiling masks. The contrast between them and her was striking and no doubt intended.

Her eyes and mouth were zipped up for her tottering descent down a set of stairs into what she assumed was an internal garage, where she was bundled into the boot of a car.

They drove for about half an hour before they stopped again. She was taken out of the boot and led by her leash chain, tottered blindly across crunchy gravel through what felt like cool night air into some kind of house. She could hear people chattering all about her and her cheeks burned at the thought of them seeing every intimate part of her exposed like this. It was so shameful and so very arousing. She felt her nipples standing up and her pussy wetting. Crystal would not be denied…

Then the flaps over her eyes were unzipped.

Angela saw she was in a large room with high curtained windows, suggesting some kind of country house ballroom.   Dozens of smartly dressed and strangely masked people were there with their slaves. It was a shocking contrast between their naked flesh of pink and olive and brown, mingling with glittering dresses and expensive fabrics. And everywhere of there were chains and leashes and cuffs and collars.

A master, mistress and slave ball, with real slaves! She never imagined there were so many of them. It was a shock to see them all together like this, without any trace of shame at what they were doing. And yet how perfectly logical it was that they'd like to gather and party, she thought, feeling sick.

Jack and Jill led her around the room talking to various people they knew, addressing by their dungeon names, and being addressed the same way in return. She would never know who these people really were under their masks or where this place was.   That was her guarantee for a safe return home, she reminded herself. Ignorance was freedom…

Angela attracted admiring glances. Many hands tweaked and probed and patted her exposed flesh, while Jack and Jill boasted modestly of her passionate responses to beating and screwing.

'Yes, she was quite a find,' Jack said casually.

And Angela felt sick and confused and yet strangely elated at this strange praise.

'What about having a bit of fun and coupling her with my girl,' a man wearing a Union Jack face mask and who called himself "Albion" said suddenly.

His girl was a lovely black girl called Cocoa, who seemed to wearing nothing but silver chains and piercings. Silver cuffs and collars confined her wrists and hobbled her ankles.

In one corner of the big room there was an oval table with a padded top, apparently intended for such things. People gathered round it as she and Cocoa were helped up onto it. Angela's mouth was unzipped and her

89

black lipped tongue clamp was removed. Albion took off the muzzle that had covered Cocoa's mouth.

'On top or underneath?' he asked.

'I think Crystal's better underneath,' Jack said.

Jack and Jill positioned Angela on her back with her legs spread and Cocoa was made to kneel over her, with her groin hovering over Angela's face while she looked down at Angela's bare pussy. She settled down over her, her brown thighs spreading around Angela's rubber clad head so that her sooty cleft parted about her nose and mouth.

Angela slid out her tongue and penetrated the girl's pussy, thankful for the practice Lady Syn had given her, even as Cocoa's lips kissed her own pussy. The heat and smell of her was overwhelming. Cocoa's tongue slid into her pussy and she surrendered to it...

Brief sudden doubt shook her. How could she do such an intimate thing in front of all these people with another slave?

No, Crystal seemed to cry out in her mind, that's exactly how she should do it. The only way to do it: as a slave and revelling in it!

Passionately Cocoa squirmed about on top of her, the pair of them coupling frantically under the gaze of all those masked eyes. She felt her loins filling with passion, while her nipples stood up like little bullets, digging into Cocoa's stomach. They were each burrowing into the others groins, their pussy lips sucking about their cheeks and noses with their clits straining, while pungent juices dripped about them.

Angela's bare bottom bounced on the table top as her loins burst and an orgasm tore through her. Cocoa reciprocated with an equally passionate thrust of her hips as each of them doused the other with their juices. Then trembling they lay still, soaking in each other's wet animal warmth.

They would never speak or know each other's true names or in all likelihood ever meet again, but they would always be joined by this intense moment of public intimacy.

Angela heard the applause and laughter and felt a sudden inexplicable surge of pleasure and pride where there should have been shame and humiliation.

* * *

In the early hours of the morning, after the slave ball, Angela was back in Jack and Jill's playroom. They were celebrating both their success and Crystal's.

Angela lay on her back with her legs doubled back under her and her wrists cuffed to ankles, with her hips raised by a vinyl covered foam rubber restraint block. A blindfold strap covered her eyes, so that her master and mistress could dispense with their masks.

Jill knelt naked over her, with her head in Angela's raised groin, enjoying the pleasures of her pussy much as Cocoa had hours before. Angela's head rested between Jill thighs, but she was not pleasuring her pussy.

Jack knelt behind his wife, thrusting his cock into that orifice. Angela kissed and licked the underside of his shaft as he pumped away, with his ball sack scraping across her nose and forehead.

Jack groaned and Jill shuddered as he happily deposited his spurted sperm up inside her. Then Jack lay across Jill's back and together they settled down over Angela to recover. She groaned under their combined weight. Slowly Jill's expelled juices and Jack's sperm began to dribble out of her plugged pussy over Angela's face. But of course, she said nothing. This was what she, at least what Crystal, was there for: to be used, to be shown off…

After coupling with Cocoa, she had attracted a lot of interest. Jill had pulled her rubber mask off and she had been examined and handled by many curious masked

91

men and women. Then somebody had wanted her to couple with their girl, a busty blonde called "Titty".

They had been hung by their wrists from the crossbar of an upright frame with four supporting struts, a little like the things swings were hung from. They were face-to-face, so that they looked into each other's eyes while their breasts pressed together. Then their pussies were joined by a big double ended dildo. Their legs had been spread out to the lower ends of the frame struts and fastened by bungee cords about their ankles, allowing them some freedom of movement.

Jack and Titty's owner had beaten their outward facing bottoms with canes, so that they jerked forward by instinct and reflex, grinding their hips against each other as they met and bounced off each other, flattening their hot sweaty breasts together and impaling each other deeper on the dildo. Then they were pulled apart by the bungee cords. Angela recalled looking into Titty's face and had seen through her tears her look of despair and repulsion at what was being done to her, and yet also a fleeting sense of wild excitement. They were the centre of attention, the stars of the show; the most important things in the room! They counted for something! And then a powerful mutual orgasm had overwhelmed both of them…

'Several people asked where we got Crystal from,' Jack said with pride. 'I didn't say she was just a hot potato that we'd come across almost by chance.'

'She was certainly a cut above the other girls there,' Jill agreed. 'She looks so fresh and natural. Just broken in, still feeling resentful and yet also obedient. It's a lovely combination.'

'And so passionate,' Jack agreed. 'You saw the way she was with that black girl. You can't teach that. It has to be something inside them…'

'I want to keep her,' Jill said suddenly.

'You know she's got an expiry date,' Jack reminded her regretfully. 'At most it would be another ten days. Then we'd have to get rid of her properly, which will cost us even more time and money. We can't risk keeping her after that.'

Jill sighed regretfully. 'I know. Well then, let's pass her on while there's plenty of interest in her and we can still get a good price…'

Then Angela knew she was going to be moving again.

Chapter Ten

Her new master went by the name of "Lord Hanuman".

From what she could see of his skin and build, he was an Indian or at least Middle Eastern man, perhaps in his forties, who wore loose white robes and a colourful papier-mâché face mask of a monkey wearing a gold crown. He kept her in what appeared to be a large converted garden shed with heavily lagged walls and misty plastic double glazed windows. The folded forms of several intricate wooden devices rested against the walls. They showed plenty of signs of wear, no doubt the result of their use on the bodies of previous slave girls.

By now Angela had stopped worrying about where she was. She might be in the next street to her own home or in another county. When you were a slave without any chance of escape that was not important. She just had to understand and then survive the whims and caprices of her new master. That was all mattered...

'Now it's my turn to monkey with you, White Woman,' Lord Hanuman told her gleefully, in a voice that combined both humour and a dash of resentful malice. 'This is my little world and you will obey my rules in here...'

She was standing before him gagged and bound by straps about her arms, which were folded up behind her back, thighs, knees and ankles. He had put a fresh deep thick leather collar on her which was hooked at the back to a rope hanging from a wooden beam spanning the sides of the shed.

He walked around her, stroking her body with his lean strong fingers, occasionally prodding and pinching. He flicked her nipples and patted her buttocks and stroked the smooth furrow of her vulva. She squirmed and whimpered at its touch, feeling her nipples and pussy responding in a perverse way that was becoming the norm. Normal for Crystal, that was.

He cupped and squeezed her breasts, pushing them together to increase her cleavage. All the time he was looking into her eyes to see how her expression changed.

'What does it feel like to have an Indian man handling you like this, White Woman?' he asked

No different from any other man who had handled during this nightmare, she thought honestly, even as she felt her nipples pressing hard into his palms. Right now, his race was the least of her worries. It was only a concern if it mattered to him…

She whimpered and moaned and chomped on her gag until he looked at her curiously.

'You want to say something?' he asked.

She nodded.

'You know that screaming won't do you any good? This building is quite soundproof.'

She nodded again.

'You will call me Lord Hanuman and you will speak politely, you understand?'

She nodded.

He undid the strap across her face and pulled out her gag.

'Please just do whatever you want to me, Lord Hanuman,' she said meekly but firmly. 'I don't care that you're brown skinned and I'm white. I'm quite helpless and you know it and I know it. That's all that matters. You're going to do sexual and sadistic things to me because you enjoy it and I can't stop you. But please don't do it because you want to take some kind of revenge for any racist insults you might have suffered in the past. I'm not responsible for those and nothing I suffer now will change them one jot. At least enjoy me honestly, as a woman in the power of a masterful man. And my name is Crystal, not "white woman"…'

She felt dizzy after making her statement. She had admitted her total helplessness! But it had to be said.

He looked at her with apparent surprise for a moment. And then he laughed.

'It seems you are an intelligent woman who can speak her mind, Crystal,' he said. 'You're different from most other girls I've entertained. But that doesn't mean I shall be any gentler with you...'

'I wasn't asking for mercy or expecting you to go easier on me, Lord Hanuman. But whatever you do, don't do it out of hate or resentment.'

'But I like the idea of tormenting you. You are the ideal of an English white woman. It excites me to dominate you. It is a fine game. A reversal of old roles, yes?'

'You can play any *game* you want with me, Lord Hanuman. That's quite a different thing. And you can make me scream and sob and beg all you like. You can make me play any part you want, take any pleasure you want. But not to pay for past wrongs.'

He laughed again. 'Very well, Crystal, you have spoken and I have listened. Now you will be silent...' he stuffed her gag back in.

'Know that I am your Indian monkey Lord who likes to play games with careless white women who have fallen into his power, because he enjoys seeing them cry.' He slapped and squeezed her bare breasts again. 'I think these should suffer...' he fingered her pussy '... but this must not be neglected. What shall I put you in? Ah, yes, this should do...'

Angela twisted round under her suspending rope to watch as he unfolded and rolled out into the middle of the room one of the devices resting against the walls. It was a narrow horizontal wooden rack on an elaborate folding base. It had vertical pillory boards, with holes cut into them for wrists and ankles, at its top and bottom ends. The top board was mounted on hollow channels through which a pair of long metal screw shafts ran, each of which had handles mounted on them at the head end of the rack. Half of the bed of the rack had wooden slats underneath it, while the rest was open. In the middle of the foot board, which was solidly bolted to the rack frame, there was a metal sleeve mounting.

Threaded horizontally through this was a metal rod which was smooth for most of its length with a short length of screw thread on the section preceding a crank handle at the foot of the table. On the other end of the rod jutting out over the open half of the rack was some kind of elaborate dildo. It had some odd fittings around its base.

Hung on hinged arms on the inside face of the head pillory board were a couple of black metal rings that seemed to carry half a dozen small metal spring-sided cups, all angled slightly inwards.

Angela gulped. The basic function of the rack was obvious enough, and even the screw rod, but what were those ring fittings for?

Lord Hanuman unhooked her from her suspending rope and made her shuffle across the floor to lie down on the rack with her torso supported by its slatted upper half. He freed her legs from their binding straps and pulled them apart and dropped her ankles into the slots in the bottom half of the pillory foot board and close the upper half over them, leaving her feet protruding from the ends of the rack. He freed her bound arms and pulled them up over her head and pushed her wrists into the slots in the upper pillory board which he also locked into place. Now she was spread out along the length of the rack with her bottom overhanging the last of the slats and her legs spread across the open gap in the rack bed. The jutting metal rod was angled up between her spread thighs in line with her bare pussy.

Hanuman went to the crank handles at the top of the table and turned them. The upper pillory board which was clamped about her wrists slid through its guide grooves up the table, pulling on her hands and stretching her body out until her feet were jammed against the holes in which her ankles were clamped and she was drawn out taut. As her shoulder sockets were pulled upwards, lifting her collar bones, the flesh and muscles of her chest were stretched, drawing out and elongating her breasts. She whimpered and bit on her gag as it felt as if she would snap.

Just then Lord Hanuman stopped cranking the handles.

He stroked her taut body appreciatively and smiled at her contorted features. 'That is how I like to see my women,' he said.

He pulled out the hinged arms supporting the curious metal rings and positioned them over, but not touching, her breasts.

He went down to the crank handle connected to the rod in the base board of the rack and it screwed it upwards until the head of the dildo pushed into her vagina. It opened up her passageway and plugged her full. Then she yelped as the fittings on the base of the dildo met her bare flesh lips. It was a ring of small spikes. Looking down her taut body, she saw it also had a row of three spring cups fitted to its top side which were all angled slightly forward.

Lord Hanuman pulled out a small drawer built into the head end of the rack and took some objects out of it. They were a gas lighter and fifteen short thick red candles.

Angela's eyes bulged as she saw them and realized what they were for. She tried to struggle but she was clamped to the rack too tightly.

Lord Hanuman fitted the candles into their ring clips so they hung over her breasts, six to each. The last three candles went into the clips over her plugged pussy. Then he clicked on the gas lighter and lit the candles.

Fifteen flames burned over the most intimate parts of her body. Because the candles were all angled inwards, and their burning wicks were close together sharing their heat, they began to melt and drip almost immediately. Angela yelped and sobbed and snivelled as splashes of hot wax fell over her breasts and shaven pussy. The hot wax streams flowed like lava down the sides of her breasts and pussy mound. It was almost as if it was erupting from her body. As it did so it burned and stung her most sensitive flesh. She sobbed and whimpered and strained at the boards holding her prisoner, tears streaming down the sides of her head.

Concentrated together as they were, the candles melted far more quickly than usual, falling in a steady rain over her. Her nipples stood up hard as they were engulfed. She could feel the wax flowing into the gaping cleft of her pussy and over her clitoris, encasing it in its scalding grip. It enveloped the rubber dildo embedded in her vagina. The wax dripping down the sides of her breasts pooled in the valley between them while it ran down their outer sides across her ribs and onto the slats under her back. The overspill around her groin ran between her spread thighs and dripped onto the floor.

Lord Hanuman watched happily as her breasts and pussy mound were covered in a glossy red casing, while she squirmed and sobbed in pain, feeling the heat of fresh drips and streams of wax burning through her.

Finally, the candles burned down to their stubs and Hanuman put them out. By then a rough red shell a centimetre thick in places covered her breasts and groin.

Angela shuddered as the flames died and slowly the heat contained within the wax flowed away, leaving it clinging to her flesh.

Lord Hanuman folded the ring support arms away from her breasts and tapped the hard wax shells and watched her wince in response.

'White women can't take a little heat, I see,' he said mockingly.

He produced a small hammer began to tap her wax covered breasts, breaking off lumps of wax. They shivered wobbled as he struck them. He hit harder and they dimpled inwards, wobbling and shivering. Her hot buried nipples were freed and stood up hard, throbbing with relief.

He moved to the foot of the rack and began turning the dildo shaft handle back and forth quickly. The spiked ring still dug into her flesh kept the candles in place over her pussy, but it was loose enough to allow the dildo shaft to pump up and down and churn inside her pussy. The movement cracked the crust of wax over it. It fell away in shards, revealing her blotched mottled skin underneath.

She surrendered pain for primitive pleasure. The juices that had been sealed in by the wax suddenly spurted out of her. She realized how hot her pussy was inside. The last shards of wax cracked off her clitoris and it swelled once more.

Then he reversed the handle quickly, pulling the dildo out of her. She yelped as the spiked ring carrying the candle stubs was torn out of her. He pulled the rod free, clearing the space between her thighs. He ducked under the end of the rack and stood between them, parting his white robes to expose a straining brown penis.

Then he picked up something else. It was a long fat red candle, which for some reason had a length of fine wire dangling from it. He rubbed its end significantly through her dripping cleft, making her groan.

'Next time I will put this up inside you and set light to it, or you could have me instead,' he told her. 'What would you rather?'

She lifted her head and stared at his cock, jerking and pleading with her eyes.

He took of her and rammed the shaft up into her desperate vagina. She took the shaft of brown flesh inside her gratefully, clinging to it tightly. Better a hundred cocks than more hot wax.

The rack creaked and shook as he rammed into her making her hot scorched breasts shiver and heave. He reached forward and squeezed her tender breasts and then slapped them and then pinched and tweaked and lifted her nipples.

She moaned and whimpered and sobbed again and squeezed on him as tightly she could.

His sperm spurted up into her and it was such a relief that it was only at blood heat that she gasped and sprayed out her juices over him.

* * *

When he had taken his pleasure from her, Lord Hanuman stepped out of the rack. He brought over a bucket and hung it on a hook screwed into the underside of the last supporting slat over which her groin hung.

'You will stay in the rack as long as I desire,' he told her.

He fed Angela some water and biscuits and then put her gag back in. She realized the light was fading in the windows. How long had she been in here?

Then Hanuman took up the long fat red candle again and pushed it up into her pussy, so that it jutted up out from between her thighs like an improbable red penis. He pulled the wires attached to the candle close to its base along her upper body and clipped their ends to her nipples, which stretched out and down as they took a little of its weight and helped hold it inside her.

'I will leave this up you overnight.' He used the gas lighter to light it. 'It will burn slowly for many hours. It should not reach your pussy lips before I come back again…'

101

She whimpered as she stared down her body at the flame on the tip of the wax shaft jutting out of her. She had become a living candleholder!

'I shall have more fun with you tomorrow, Crystal,' he told her.

Then he left her in the shed for the night. As the light left the room, she only had the candle flame for company.

* * *

Afterwards it seemed incredible to Angela that she had been able to fall asleep while stretched out within a rack with a burning candle plugged into her pussy. But, after watching it for an hour, desperately calculating how fast it was burning and deciding it really would last for several hours more, she was so exhausted that even such fear and discomfort was not enough to stop her drifting off. At least she was lying on her back. But inevitably there was a price to pay. That night she had terrible dreams of being buried naked in hot wax, while flames danced on her nipples.

* * *

When she was aroused the next morning by Lord Hanuman coming back into the shed and she tried to move, she found her arms and legs were stiff as boards and felt dead after being stretched out so tightly. Her hands and feet were cold and numb from the boards clamped about her wrists and ankles. Her stretched nipples were also numbed where the wires had tugged on them. But at least the strain had steadily diminished during the night. The big candle was still alight but it still had few centimetres to go before it reached her pussy.

Hanuman freed the clips from her nipples and pulled the candle out of her. She shuddered with relief as her vagina contracted slowly.

She had hoped he would now free her from the rack, but that was not the case.

He gave her more food and water and wiped her over with a cold flannel. And then he adjusted the mountings of the rack, tilting its bed and her until she was vertical, with her back lifting clear of the slats on which she had been resting. The bucket swung out between her legs.

'Empty your wastes into your bucket,' he told her.

Snivelling and with her cheeks burning, she did so. He uncoiled a garden hose plugged into a tap in the corner of the shed and flushed her groin clean. The cold water eased her stretched and aching pussy.

He removed the bucket and then twisted the slats in their mounting grooves until they came free, leaving her hanging within an open rectangular wooden frame, with her wrists and ankles clamped at it top and bottom ends. He unclamped her ankles from the lower restraining board, which he then unbolted and pulled out of its mounting slots, leaving her numbed feet dangling a few inches above the floor. She kicked them about as her whole weight was taken by her clamped wrists.

'Would you like something to stand on?' he asked.

She whimpered and nodded frantically.

He pushed a heavy metal grill panel mounted on short legs under her feet so she could stand on it. Then he brought out a pair of heavy bungee cords and looped and hooked their ends about her breasts and hung their other ends over hooks screwed into the top board of the rack.

What was he doing now?

He opened up the split board enough to pull her by now numbed hands out of it. Angela shrieked and sobbed as her stiff shoulders were bent downward and twisted about for the first time in many hours. He cuffed her wrists behind her back, leaving her swaying within the frame of the rack, held upright only by the bungee cords about her breasts.

103

He cranked the adjustable top board of the rack a little higher, increasing the tension on the bungee cords so that her breasts were squeezed into pink and purple balloons of flesh and then dragged up her chest.

Then he produced something else: a shallow metal tray set out with two dozen night light candles. He took out the gas lighter and lit them, while Angela watched first with puzzlement and then growing horror. When all the candles were alight, he bent and slid it under the grill on which she was standing. As the heat of the massed candle flames struck the soles of her feet she began to skip about madly to avoid them being scorched.

'I thought it appropriate that a hot potato should feel the heat,' Hanuman said.

If she stepped off the grating, there was nothing else to stand on and she would be dangling solely from her bound breasts.

'Now you will dance for me, Crystal,' he said, pulling up a chair and sitting down to watch.

And dance Angela did, skipping about frantically, lifting one foot and then the other, hopping and twisting about, struggling to keep her balance even as the metal of the grill began to burn the bottoms of her feet. This only increased the strain on her bound breasts, which were turning purple before her very eyes as they jiggled and wobbled and bunched up as the bungee cords threatened to throttle them. Her tears of pain splashed onto their glossy upper slopes.

After a few minutes of this sadistic spectacle, Hanuman said. 'There is one way to put the flames out of course: with lots of water. You could provide it yourself, if I had not got you to empty yourself out earlier. Still if you beg me to feed you more...'

She groaned and nodded frantically.

He had squeezy bottle of water with a short plastic tube attached to it. He pulled out her gag and pushed it into her mouth and she sucked it down desperately, even

104

while she kept dancing with her feet. He smiled and squeezed and slapped her bulging breasts as she drank.

By the time she had guzzled over a litre of water she felt drunk and dizzy and her stomach was bulging. He pulled the tube out of her mouth and gagged her again.

She still had to keep dancing while the water worked its way through her, trying to save her feet from being scorched. She was snorting in air like a race horse and sweating from the strain. Lord Hanuman got up and walked around her, admiring the way the flesh of her buttocks with shivering as she pumped up and down. He stroked his fingers through her sweaty cleft. She had been turned into his pain puppet: there to dance for his amusement.

Finally, Angela felt her bladder filling. She bowed her legs wide, standing with her tiptoes on the corners of the grill, and peed over the flames under her, twisting and squirming her hips about to squirt the jet out of her like a fire hose. There was a hiss of steam and the candle flames were extinguished.

She sagged limply, able to stand on the cooling iron grill at last.

Lord Hanuman applauded. 'Very good,' he said. 'What a spectacle you made. I'll just relight the candles and we'll do it again…'

Angela shrieked and sobbed and shook her head, pleading with her eyes. No, not that again!

'Have you something else to offer to entertain me?' Hanuman asked.

Angela wiggled her bottom, sticking it out suggestively as far as she could.

'Are you offering me the pleasures of your backside?'

She nodded.

He extended the bungee cords bound about her breasts, allowing her to stand on the floor, spread her

105

legs and bend forward with the bungee cords over her shoulders, pushing her bottom out. He removed the grill and tray of extinguished candles so he could stand close to her and examine her sweaty bottom.

'This has not had much attention so far, but it is pleasingly formed,' he observed. 'Are its depths hot and pleasing?'

She nodded, feeling dizzy with a growing sense of sick fear and excitement.

'Do you think it could do with a beating to warm it further first?'

She nodded. Of course, she had to be beaten...

He took a wooden paddle down from where it hung on a nail on the wall and stroked across her buttocks. Then he swished it hard, smacking into them and making them wobble and shiver, even as the sharp report of wood striking flesh echoed about the shed. Angela yelped and snivelled from the pain, jerking forward slightly and tugging on her bound breasts, but she kept her legs spread wide and her bottom offered up invitingly.

He delivered half a dozen more blows to each buttock cheek until they were rosy red. The pain caused her to spurt out a little more pee onto the floor.

Then Hanuman dropped the paddle and felt between her legs, scooping up some of her pussy dribble and rubbing it into the pucker of her anus. Then he ripped open his robes and rammed his hard brown penis between her burning bottom cheeks until her sphincter gave way before it so it could slide up into her rectum.

Holding onto her hips, he rammed into her with bruising force setting her body swaying and tugging on her bound breasts. The elastic resistance of the bungee cords kept pulling her back, impaling her onto him again. There was no escape.

Then he grunted and shot his seed out into her hot tight interior and she felt such a swell of relief that the shudder of a sympathetic orgasm course through her. Temporarily spent, he bent forward over her and rested, and she had no choice but to support him on her back, his weight stretching the bungee cords further and strangling her breasts again.

After some minutes, he asked. 'What else can you offer me?'

Exhausted and dizzy, she grunted and whimpered until he pulled her gag out again.

'When you have recovered, I will suck you off, Lord Hanuman,' she said humbly, hoping this little bit of playacting would appeal to him. 'I will take you in my mouth and swallow your sperm down and suck you off afterwards like a humble slave should.'

'You will do all this for my brown penis?'

'I will do anything for my Master's penis, Lord,' she said solemnly.

And when he was recovered, he moved his chair round to position it under her bowed head. With him holding her by her hair to keep her face ground against his lap, she did suck him off until he spouted down her throat. It burned but she swallowed it down. And after she had licked him clean, he wiped his shaft dry on her hair.

It was an act of total humiliating surrender: somehow both terrible and perfect at the same time. Of course, it was Crystal's act of surrender, not hers…

* * *

Angela was so exhausted she was falling asleep even bent over bound by her breasts with her hands cuffed up behind her and her face resting in his lap. Lord Hanuman slapped her cheeks to rouse her, and then lifted her head up so she could look him in the eye.

'I have humbled you, I have abused you and you have submitted. You have been properly defiled. There is only one final indignity I can put you to. I shall now sell you on for money, just like I would any other piece of property…'

Chapter Eleven

They called themselves "The Harpies."

They were two plump early-middle-aged women who wore black witch's robes and bat masks to conceal their identities. They referred to each other as "Lobelia" and "Hyacinth", which may or may not have been their true names. Perhaps they were sisters or lesbian lovers or simply good friends sharing a perverted taste for keeping other women as slaves.

By rights, The Harpies should have operated out of some of gloomy hollow in the woods, or at least a cobwebbed kitchen with a huge pot bubbling over an open hearth, but in fact they kept Angela in a big old-fashioned iron frame greenhouse. There was an exposed sandy bed down the middle of the greenhouse which had a garden table and a pair of chairs set out upon it, with a path of stone slabs around it serving several potting tables, cluttered with plants and shrubs, assorted empty plant pots and gardening tools. There was a garden tap and hose in one corner. All the greenhouse windows were covered by whitewash, so that she could not see out and nobody from outside, assuming there was anybody there, could look in to watch her suffering. That was reserved exclusively for Lobelia and Hyacinth, who arranged it with perverse ingenuity and with a horticultural bent.

So far they had done nothing violent to her, but their interests were clearly so peculiar that Angela felt more disturbed by them than anybody else who had so far owned her. Not that there was anything she could do about it, of course. They might seem like bumbling eccentric women, but they had taken no chances over her restraints.

Angela stood in the middle of the sandy bed in a big terracotta plant pot buried almost up to her knees in gravel. She stood very straight because of the end of a broomstick, also buried in the pot, which was bound with garden wire to the backs of her knees and ankles, was lodged up her rear passage. Her arms were tied behind her back with shrub tie straps. A ball of soft coated garden wire plugged her mouth.

Lobelia and Hyacinth, carrying wooden trug baskets, were fussing around her turning her into a living plant. They had pieces of coloured soft plastic cut into the shapes of leaves and petals, already fitted with self adhesive patches, which they were sticking on her. They had ringed her face and breasts with circles of petals, with a smaller ring of petals stuck around each nipple. Her nipples had stood up while the women applied the petals, much to their amusement.

'I see her buds are rising all by themselves,' Hyacinth observed.

A large plastic flower head peeped out of the cleft of her pussy, the lips of which had fans of green leaves stuck to them. The stalk of another flower had been threaded through the ball of wire in her mouth so that it appeared to blossom from between her lips. Now they were sticking larger green plastic leaves in her hair and making them appear to sprout out of the cleft of her buttocks.

Finally, when they were done they stepped back to admire the transformation they had wrought.

'Doesn't she look lovely,' Lobelia said.

'She looks like a most exotic flower,' Hyacinth agreed. She bent to sniff delicately at Angela's pussy, which had been stimulated by having the stalk of a plastic plant the stuck up it and was dripping down her thighs. 'And so delightfully scented as well...'

'It's just a pity that the winds must blow and petals and leaves must fall,' Lobelia said regretfully.

'Yes, it's a pity that it has to happen,' Hyacinth agreed, 'but that's nature's way...'

They put their trug baskets on the potting tables and took up two stout bamboos which had long trailing bunches of heavy green garden string tied to their ends. As they circled around Angela, they swished them about through the air.

'I hear the wind rising,' Lobelia said.

'So do I, Dear,' Hyacinth agreed.

Angela cringed, feeling sudden fear fill her.

The two women swiped their bamboo and string lashes across Angela's body. They smacked and rasped across her skin, ripping at the plastic leaves and petals the two women had so carefully positioned. Under the onslaught they were ripped off her body while her exposed flesh stung and burned as it was beaten.

Angela yelped and squirmed, churning the broom handle in her bottom, while plastic petals flew all about her as the string lashes swished and cracked and cut across her. The plant in her mouth was ripped out as was the one in her pussy. The rings of petals about her nipples were swiped off even as her nipples were beating down, leaving her breasts shaking and trembling.

The spray of leaves erupting from her clenching buttocks were now attacked by the "wind" and was torn out and scattered, while the upper slopes of her bottom stung and burned. As the petals and leaves vanished, they were replaced by criss-cross blotches of fine red stripes where she been beaten.

The onslaught only stopped when every petal and leaf had been torn off her body. Angela stood in the pot shivering and trembling. Now she was truly denuded, without even a plastic fig leaf to cover herself.

The two women inspected the damage they had done, stroking and pinching her all over. They felt the heat in her buttocks and tweaked her nipples and slid their fingers up into her pussy cleft, testing how hot and wet and slippery she was. Angela squirmed and shivered as they pawed her all over. She wished they would just get on and screw her, if that was what they wanted to do.

But they had even more perverse games in mind…

* * *

Angela whimpered as she braced herself painfully at one end of the sandpit.

She was supporting her upper body more or less level with the ground, with her shoulders twisted and her arms straight under her and her legs splayed and knees bent. There were plant ties about her wrists and ankles that were bound to stakes driven deep into the sand, keeping her feet and hands in position. To ease the strain of such a posture, even if she could not move her feet and hands, she would simply have sat down. She could not do that because there was a pot of cactuses under her bottom.

There was also a plastic funnel taped into her mouth and another piece of tape went over her nostrils, forcing her to breathe through the funnel. Hyacinth was holding a jug of water tinted green by food dye which she was pouring into the funnel. Angela had to drink it down to continue to breathe. She was ready exhausted and her stomach was sloshing. It was a little like the torment Lord Hanuman had put her through, but in a strange way more sporting.

Her open legs faced along the length of the sandpit. There were green splatters radiating out from between her legs in the sand and little plastic plant markers pushed into the sand at the end of each splattered trail like little flags. Lobelia stood beside the sandpit holding more of the markers.

'Ready to have another go?' Hyacinth asked sweetly.

Miserably, Angela nodded, screwing up her eyes anticipation.

Hyacinth positioned herself and then pushed her flat hand down sharply over Angela's bulging lower

112

stomach. This forced her bottom down onto the bowl of cacti. As she howled through the funnel still taped her mouth, her bladder cut loose due to the sudden pain and pressure. Her urine came out in a green spurt from her cleft and jetted in a sparkling arc across the sand to splash down a good three metres away.

When the jet subsided to a dribble running down the cleft of her pussy onto the sand between her legs, Lobelia stepped forward and placed a fresh marker in the sand.

'You beat your previous best by a good four inches, Crystal,' she declared. 'Come on; let's see if we can get it to the end of the bed…'

Wincing, Angela strained her trembling arms and legs to lift herself off the cacti, feeling even more tiny spines embedded in her buttock cheeks. Her bottom felt like a pincushion and she thought her shoulders and hips and knees were going to snap from the strain. But there was no escape.

Hyacinth began pouring more green water into the funnel…

* * *

By the time the peeing game ended, Angela could hardly move.

Her joints ached from the strain of supporting herself in that unnatural position. At least the funnel had been removed from her mouth. Then Hyacinth and Lobelia had great fun bending her over their laps so they could use tweezers to pull the cacti spines out of her stinging bottom. Surely, they had finished with her for the day? But soon she found that she had one more ordeal to undergo…

The women knelt her down on the sand with her wrists once again strapped up behind her back. Then they showed her a shovel with a strangely shaped handle. On the end of the shaft, set on a swivel mount, was a large rubber dildo with a second curving prong

113

underneath it with a bulbous cap on the end. Connected to a ring screwed halfway down the shaft was a length of wire cored rope which ended in a large pear-shaped rubber plug.

'We want you to dig a pit in the sand with this shovel,' Hyacinth told her.

'But we don't want you to use your hands to do it,' Lobelia added.

They plugged the handle of the shovel up into her groin. The ribbed dildo forced her vagina open and then clung inside her, while the curving plug underneath it was pushed up into her bottom until its head popped through the ring of her sphincter, which when it closed about its tapering neck locked itself in place. The pear-shaped plug on the end of the wire was pushed between her teeth, filling her mouth. Now the shovel lay on the sand in front of the, jutting out of her groin. She could fill the weight of it pulling on her insides.

The Harpies made her get up. As she did so the end of the shovel flopped downwards until the wire connected to the plug in her mouth tightened. If she moved her head up and down, the end of the shovel moved as well.

'Dig here,' Lobelia told her, drawing an "X" in the sand with the toe of her boot. Both women also had their bamboo garden string lashes on their hands and she didn't need to be told how they would be used to encourage her.

Awkwardly, Angela began to dig.

Every thrust of her hips to drive the shovel into the sand churned the plugs in her pussy and rectum. Then she had to strain with her neck and shoulders to lift the end of the shovel with a load of sand on its end, which she had to tip to one side. It was only possible to work like this because the sand was dry and find. Even so, the strain on her back and neck was incredible, and after ten minutes they were throbbing and aching. But there was no letup.

It was fine for the women watching her, who sat beside a garden table sipping iced orange juice.

'You'll have your glass when you've finished,' Lobelia promised her.

Down and down she went, sweating profusely in the still air of the greenhouse. The drips fell off her nipples as she bent over to pull out the next spade-full, and ran down the cleft of her buttocks and into her plugged groin. Her hair was sodden and her neck and thighs were on fire, but still she dug.

Suddenly the twisting, pumping and grinding of the ribbed dildo in her pussy became too much, or perhaps her body was acting in self defence. Angela felt the spasm of an orgasm overwhelm her and she dropped her knees and hunched over, squeezing the shaft of the shovel between her thighs.

For a few seconds, she was lost in orgasmic bliss. Then string lashes beat down across her back.

'No rest until you finished!' the Harpies shouted.

Sobbing and trembling, Angela got back onto her feet and continued digging, now with orgasmic juices dripping down the shaft of the shovel.

* * *

The pit was almost a metre deep when the Harpies finally called a halt.

Angela sank to her knees, whimpering and panting for breath. Her legs felt like flayed rubber while her back seemed ready to break. The Harpies brought over an old garden chair and a large plant pot. The chair had no seat to it.

They pulled the terrible spade plug handle out of her pussy and anus, dripping with her juices. The anal plug came free with a pop. She felt bruised inside.

Good as their word, the Harpies gave Angela a glass of iced orange juice to drink, which she gulped down greedily. Then they pushed the regular ball gag into her mouth to take the place of the spade plug she had been holding in there for hours. Then they pointed at pit.

'Kneel down inside that,' they told her.

Fearful and mystified, she obeyed.

Using regular shovels, the Harpies quickly filled in the hole around her until she was buried in the sand up to her neck.

They lifted up the seat-less garden chair and positioned it over her head. Then they lifted up their black skirts to reveal they had nothing on underneath them. She glimpsed chubby buttocks, sturdy thighs and plump shaven pink pussy clefts.

Lobelia sat down on the seat above Angela's head, spread her thighs to the corners of the seat and peed all over her.

Angela whimpered and spluttered in revulsion as the hot pee streamed over her. But there was no escape.

When Lobelia had finished, Hyacinth took her place and a fresh stream of pee spurted down all over her.

When she was done, she lifted the chair off Angela's head.

From a moment both women smiled sweetly down at her bedraggled and miserable face. 'Sleep well,' they said. Then they upended the big plant pot and put it over her head and left her there for the night.

* * *

It was one of the longest and most uncomfortable night's Angela had ever spent. She was helplessly confined in the sand; soiled, dirty and miserable. The grains worked their way in everywhere. After a few hours of kneeling, her legs went to sleep. And then she realized she had to pee herself. It seeped out into the sand about her groin, feeling as if she was wearing a nappy filled with sand. It was even worse when it cooled.

As sheer exhaustion overwhelmed her, her head lolled about, occasionally dropping forward and banging

against the inside of the plant pot. It was a nightmare…
a nightmare…

* * *

The plant pot being pulled off her and the glare of the scattered sunlight filtering through the whitewash windows of the greenhouse brought Angela out of her nightmare with a jerk.

Hyacinth and Lobelia were smiling down at her.

'Good morning, rise and shine,' they said brightly.

They dug her out of the pit and hauled her numbed and hunched body out onto the open sand. They sprayed her over with the garden hose, its chill water reviving her a little, even as it washed away the filth from her body.

They gave her some food and drink, and then they put a choke collar around her neck to control her. They got her onto her feet and supported her as she tottered over to one of the potting tables. They made her climb up onto it and lie on her back with her legs pulled up and spread wide. Soft coated garden ties were bound about her arms, ankles and knees to hold them in place. More loops of wire went over the insides of her thighs, and through her groin, peeling back her pussy lips to expose its pink wet depths.

When she was secured, Lobelia held up something for her to see. It was a glass jam jar filled with wriggling pink worms.

'You know how important these are to gardens to keep the soil aerated and so on,' she told Angela. 'Well we find they have very useful effects on the girls we play with as well…'

And she up-ended the jar, pushing its open rim into Angela's peeled-back pussy.

Angela shrieked and sobbed and wailed into her gag, while her body tensed as her hips lifted and she bucked in utter horror. But she had been too well tied down. She could feel the slimy things squirming into

117

her pussy and exploring its depths. They were tickling and pulsating and wriggling into her.

'Oh, look at them burrowing into her,' Lobelia said brightly.

'Burrowing all the way down,' Hyacinth agreed.

With bulging horror-filled eyes, Angela turned her head to the Harpies, pleading mutely. She'd do anything, anything else, but endure this.

'Would you like to please us in another way?' Hyacinth asked

Angela nodded her head frantically.

'Perhaps there is another game we can play with her,' Hyacinth said.

'Perhaps we could give it a go…' Lobelia agreed.

* * *

Angela knelt on the sand in front of the Harpies as they sat back in their garden chairs, sipping their orange juice. The skirts were rolled up, exposing their plump pink pussies. Her own pussy had been cleaned out of the worms, only to be plugged with the closed blades of a pair of garden shears, turned upside down so that its handles angled downwards in an inverted V and were braced on the sand between her thighs.

The cold metal blades, even closed, felt frightening and dangerous as they filled her tender vagina.

But she didn't mind.

Her anus was plugged with the handle end of a lighter and longer hoe, which rested above the shears and whose end was wedge in the sand behind her.

But she didn't mind.

Angela was shifting from left to right and dipping her head between one swollen pussy and the other, licking and lapping and sucking at them desperately. The two handles churned uncomfortably inside her every time she moved from one pussy to the other. Helplessly, she felt her pussy dribbling about them and squeezing tentatively, as if in anticipation of them actually violating her as if they were living things.

But she didn't mind.

Every so often, the Harpies reached over with their garden string lashes and smacked her bare buttocks.

But she didn't mind.

She would play this game again, or any other game they wished all day long, as long as she didn't have to endure the worms again.

And then Angela realized what a terrible thrill it was to submit so abjectly to the power of other people.

She was no longer sure what she was thinking, or whether she was Angela or Crystal. She hated Hyacinth and Lobelia and yet she also loved them slavishly and envied the power they had over her. She was counting the minutes until, inevitably, they sold her on, also knowing at the same time that she would feel they had betrayed her, or else she had been inadequate.

Oh God, she was becoming a gutless submissive! But there was no escape… and she still had a week more to endure.

Chapter Twelve

Mister Steel was a brawny man in a work shirt, heavy boots and a leather apron. Only from the back was it apparent that he was bare from the waist down. His features were covered with an iron rivet effect mask, moulded into manlike features with slots for his eyes, nose and mouth. He had a gravelly voice in keeping with his physique and the mask.

Angela had woken up feeling sick dizzy as usual, to find herself huddled up no longer gagged but still cuffed and confined in a cage at one end of his spacious well stocked workshop. It was fitted out with a lathe, a metal press, bench drills and vices, jig saws and a welding kit and all the other tools of a worker of both metal and wood. Blinds covered the windows. The workshop smelt of wood shavings, oil and hot metal. Bizarrely, there were also a couple of very worn and battered female shop window mannequins hung on the walls. They had clearly been fitted with extra joints to enable a more realistic range of movements, and also had apertures cut into them to represent vaginas and anuses.

Once he had seen she was stirring, Steel left his work to peer in through the bars the cage at her. He prodded and poked her a few times.

'You do what I tell you girl, get it?' he growled.

She nodded fearfully.

'There's water and a sandwich and a bucket there. You keep quiet and don't bother me. I'll take you out when I need you...' Then he returned to his work.

As she watched him while her head cleared, she began to get the impression that he made bondage, punishment and restraining devices to order. And of course, if his dummies were not sufficiently versatile, he needed some living slave to try them out on. Underlying her normal stomach churning fear and confusion during her first few hours in the workshop, she also felt a twinge of resentment that she had been bought first and foremost to serve as his product testing guinea pig and only secondly as a source of personal pleasure and amusement. But of course, her feelings meant nothing. Whatever function he wanted her to serve, she would do so. She felt Crystal warm at the thought. Her nipples stood up and her pussy grew hot and slippery.

This was the new normal, Crystal thought, and she had to accept and adapt to survive.

But do you need to enjoy it quite so much, Angela wondered?

Why not? I can if I want to. It's my life and my body.

Oh God, I'm arguing with myself, Angela thought. I'm going mad!

No, you're going to *sane*, Crystal suggested.

What do you mean by that?

You know. After all, you're me…

* * *

There was an open space in the middle of the floor between the two ends of the workshop. While Angela watched, Mister Steel pulled a curious device out into it and fussed over it for some time, checking it over carefully and plugging into a power socket.

It looked a bit like a wooden vaulting horse of the kind gymnasts used, but with other additions, most notably a tubular metal gibbet arm fixed to one end that overhung its middle. Some complicated device hung from its end.

When he was satisfied, he came over to her cage, opened it up and pulled her out by her hair.

'There's something I want to try out new girl,' he told her. 'And afterwards, you're going to tell me what you think of it…'

She was to be his slave product tester and reporter! He wanted what his dummies could not give him: feedback! It seemed crazy, and yet looked at coldly, it was perfectly understandable. Apparently, he took pride

121

in his work and wanted to deliver a product that performed as intended.

He pulled her over to the horse, which had a mounting block beside it. He helped her up onto it and she straddled the wooden body. Immediately she found out that it was greased and had a saw tooth ridge of rubber running down its length, like the fringe down the spine of a lizard. Some of these segments were stiffened in the middle by tapering prongs, while others had apexes that spread out forward and back to form rubber hooks. The serrations were semi-hard and bent under her weight, but nevertheless they cut into her groin, parting the lips of her pussy and probed the pucker of her anus.

He slipped her feet into what looked like metal stirrups with extra ankle straps and buckled them in place. They were hung on horizontal bars running the length of the horse's body, so they could slide freely back and forth.

Mister Steel adjusted the device hanging from the gibbet arm, which she realized now resembled the tail of the beast curving up and back over its body. There were three nooses forming a triangle, with the lower two nooses connected to the upper one and all hanging from a heavy spring. The upper noose he closed about her neck. It was padded on the inside and quite rigid so it could not squeeze tightly about her throat. The two nooses that hung from its lower curves he placed over and tightened about the roots of her breasts, making them bulge outwards.

She had a brief flashback to her breast suspension by Lord Hanuman. Not again, she thought in despair. But it wasn't quite like that…

Mister Steel walked around the horse to check she was properly secured. Then he took a small remote-control unit out of the pocket of his apron and pressed a button.

122

Motors inside the device hummed and compressed air hissed. The horse's front splayed legs, which looks to be made of ordinary adjustable nested sections, suddenly contracted, tipping its body forward. With a yelp of surprise, Angela slid forward as well. The saw tooth rubber ridge ripped through her pussy as she slid while her stirrup cuffed ankles ran down the length of their bars. Only the nooses about her neck and breasts stopped her pitching all the way forward. As it was, the spring on which they were hung stretched, pulling her head and shoulders backwards and keeping her upright. The noose about her neck tightened as it rode up under her chin, while the ones about her breasts contracted even further and pinched them tightly, pulling them up her chest even as they bulged outward. She could feel the nooses had spring or elastic cords in them which kept them in place.

Then the horse shifted under her again. Its front legs lengthened and its back legs contracted. She slid helplessly backwards along its greased top, the rubber serrations rasping through her pussy and bottom cleft again in the other direction. As she passed the mid-point, the straining eased for a fraction of a second on her throat and breasts, and then as she came to a halt over the back end of the horse, her throat was clamped and her breasts were pinched tight once more.

And so back and forth she was pitched on the bucking, dipping horse. She sobbed and yelped in alarm as she was thrown about; the rubber serrations rasping through her pussy, making it dribble and swell and helpless excitement. The prong-reinforced sections briefly pushed deep up into her as they went, while those with hammerhead hooked tips pulled and teased her flesh lips. She tried squeezing her thighs tight about the horse but it hardly made any difference.

Soon her juices had been smeared from one end of the rubber ridge piece to the other.

Then Mister Steel touched another button, and the body of horse began to vibrate as it rocked forward and back. Angela gasped and bit on her gag. It was like nothing she had ever felt before, as if it really had come to life between her thighs. She was riding a bucking Bronco sex machine! The vibrations were transmitted up through the rubber serrations wedged inside her, teasing her clit even further. Even the nipples on her intermittently half throttled breasts were standing up hard as they were squeezed and dropped and then squeezed again.

She could feel a terrible, inevitable climax approaching.

Why are you fighting it, Crystal wondered?

Why was she?

Her loins burst and she bucked and twisted frantically, kicking her cuffed legs about so that her stirrups rattled against the side bars. Then she slumped limp and exhausted over the device, only held up by the nooses around her neck and breasts.

Mister Steel did not give her long to rest. While she sat there trembling, feeling the juices of her orgasm seeping away under her thighs, he took out a note pad from a pocket in his apron. He jabbed the tip of his pencil into the underside of her bulging left breasts to shock her back into awareness.

He fired a string of questions at her. 'What are your thoughts about the horse? Was it adequately powerful... intimate... unexpected? Were the rubber fringe elements big enough... sufficiently varied in form... properly intrusive? How would you rate your overall experience of the horse out of ten...?'

And she had to clear her mind enough to give him intelligible answers. If she was slow, she would get another jab from his pencil again. The last question she found especially terrifying. Could she criticise his creativity and expect not be punished?

'I rate it as eight point five... no, no, a nine! Yes, a nine,' she said desperately.

'Was it a good orgasm?'

'Yes... it was a great orgasm... one of my best... Master,' she babbled.

Apparently satisfied, Mister Steel put away his notebook. He unfastened her from the horse and half carried her back to her cage.

'You get some rest,' he said, locking her in. 'I've got some other things I want to try out on you later...'

Angela slumped back in her cage, dazed and exhausted. It was bad enough being subjected to such devices for sadistic pleasure, without have to having to think up nice things to say about them afterwards!

* * *

The next time Steel pulled Angela out of her cage, there was an entirely new device waiting for her in the middle of the room.

There was low heavy deep table also connected to a mains power cable, sitting beneath a bar suspended from its ends by chains that extended upwards to a hook hung on a ceiling beam. There was a second smaller bar, about a third the length of the main one, dangling from its middle. It had a padded steel collar opened out in two halves fitted to its middle, and smaller cuffs on each end.

Mister Steel sat Angela on the table and laid her on her back. She saw it had a ten by ten grid dividing its top up into squares with openings underneath each section.

He lifted her legs up and cuffed her ankles to ends of the main bar, so that they were spread wide. Then he took hold of the dangling middle bar and bent her forward until she whimpered when it felt as if her hip joints were being twisted off. Now her head was level with her knees. He snapped the collar of the middle bar about her neck and its cuffs about her knees. Now she was secured doubled over, balanced on her bottom on

125

top of the strange table, with her legs extending upwards and outwards in a straining "V" which left her groin gaping.

He pointed a remote-control handset to the ceiling and some motor hummed, lifting the chains of the bar from which he dangled so that she was raised clear of the table top and hung suspended freely over it

Angela winced at the strain on the tendons down the back of her legs and was acutely aware of how exposed she was, but she was not sure what was meant to happen next. She soon found out...

Steel pressed a button on the side of the strange table, and motors purred inside it. There were hisses of compressed air and suddenly hollow rubber fingers and spikes and screw bits began popping up out of the holes and attacking her exposed buttocks and groin. At the same time, rows of coloured LED lights set between the holes began flashing, illuminating her body from below.

Some of the inflated rubber appendages had sharp plastic spikes on their tips which gouged and stabbed at her intimate parts. Others were like party blowouts that uncoiled and smacked their spiked tips against her thighs and buttocks. Those longer than the others pushed briefly up into her gaping pussy and rasped about inside it before being sucked back out again. The slimmer ones even penetrated her anus.

Together they created a relentless barrage of prodding, smacking, rasping rubber that jabbed and flailed about her dangling haunches. Sobbing and shrieking in pain and confusion, she jerked and twisted in a futile attempt to escape, only causing her body to spin and sway around above the table top, exposing more of her flesh to the onslaught. However, mingled with pain and shock was pleasure. The massive overstimulation caused her pussy to swell and begin to dribble, while her clitoris rose to the stimulation of the prodding rasping rubber fingers.

As she sobbed and jerked amidst the frothing rubber snakes engulfing her groin, Mister Steel walked around her making notes.

An unfolding blowout finger penetrated all the way up her vagina. Instinctively she clung onto it so it could not retract. It throbbed and pulsed within her trying to inflate again. But she would not let it go. As the other probes smacked and rasped and slithered about her groin, she shuddered and came over it. It was not intense but was all she could manage.

Mister Steel shut off the machine, leaving her trembling and dripping over it but still needy.

Once again he bombarded her with questions. 'Did the lights add to her experience… should he add music… was it better or worse than the horse?'

'It was different… different…' she said huskily. 'More rapidly arousing… more teasing… but the rubber bits moved so fast… yes, add music… and please screw me…'

He blinked at her in surprise. And then he put his notepad away, pushed the table to one side, reversed his apron so his swelling penis could spring out freely, took hold of her dangling body and rammed his cock up into her wet pussy.

That was what she really wanted inside her at that moment: not a bit of rubber but a real cock.

* * *

That night in the workshop, illuminated only by electric nightlights, Angela slept in a bondage coffin. There was no other word for it because that was what it looked like, except that instead of a solid lid it had one made of bar metal mesh.

The inside the coffin was comfortably padded. There were loops of heavy slotted straps that protruded inwards through slots in its slides. These were looped about Angela's wrists and ankles and then drawn tight and padlocked on the outside of the coffin. Strap loops

127

went across the top end of the coffin above and below her neck, holding her head down, and across its middle, securing her stomach.

She was almost totally immobilised, but oddly she also felt safely enclosed. The padding was deep and warm. It was almost relaxing. Except that any relaxation was only temporary and she only slept in short spells. She was still product testing for Mister Steel, even in her sleep.

There were fittings on the inside of the coffin lid over her breasts and groin. There was a pair of pneumatically operated soft rubber suckers fastened onto her breasts which pulsated as if they were part of a milking machine. A screw dildo extended down at an angle from the device over her groin and was lodged in her pussy. They were connected to some timer arranged to set the things off every couple of hours.

Angela would be jerked awake to find her breasts being massaged and sucked while her pussy was being drilled out. Helplessly she responded to the relentless stimulation as she was brought to another orgasm, which left a stain on the padding under her groin. Then the devices would go quiet and she could try to sleep again, until the next time.

Don't try to fight them, Crystal advised in her sleep.

But I'm so tired, Angela said.

Not long to go now, Crystal reminded her.

And then what, Angela wondered?

That's up to you…

* * *

The next morning in the daylight, after giving her report on the effectiveness of the coffin, Angela was soon testing another of Mister Steel's ingenious devices.

Angela's head protruded through the pillory board top of a low box frame device set on castors. The board top in front of her face had a scallop cut out of it so that a man standing in front of her could have access to her mouth, which was positioned level with his groin. Rubber hooks set on adjustable brackets on either side of her cheeks held her mouth invitingly open.

Her arms were pulled up and back, twisting her shoulders so that her hands protruded through the board on either side of her head. This kept her upper body stiffly upright within the frame. Her bottom end was secured by her rectum being impaled upon a dildo bolted to the base of the frame. Her legs were bent up at the hips and twisted and splayed out wide and her knees and ankles were strapped to the forward struts of the frame. This caused her naked groin to gape wide and open in the proper fashion. To increase her vulnerability, hooks on springs fitted the sides of the box frame, curved in underneath her splayed and stretched thighs and were fastened onto her outer labia, pulling them apart so that her pink pubic valley was open for all to see.

Just in front of her pussy was a rubber paddle covered with drawing pin-like spikes, which was actuated by a hinged rod connected to a small pedal set to one side of the front of the box.

Mister Steel stood in the scallop front of the box with toe pressed down on the pedal. The spiked paddle smacked against the soft wet inner lips of Angela's gaping pussy. She winced and whimpered as the spikes tormented her and redoubled her efforts to give pleasure. Mister Steel's cock filled her mouth and she was sucking desperately on it, while he held her loosely by her hair.

She realized her body been reduced to two orifices: her pricked and dripping pussy and her desperately sucking and gulping mouth. The ease and salvation of one depended on the activity of the other.

Right now, his cock is the most important thing in the world, Crystal said. Believe it and he'll come.

I want to be sick, Angela replied.

Do you want our pussy to be turned into a pincushion?

She could feel his moment coming even as, despite the pain, or possibly because of it, she could feel her own lust filling her loins. How could such cruelty do that to her?

He came down her throat just as her pussy sprayed her juices out over its tormenting spiked paddle. And once again, for a few precious seconds, Angela knew perfect bliss beyond doubt or reason.

* * *

'I know somebody who could make good use of a fine, juicy sub girl like you,' Mister Steel said afterwards, while his softening cock was still in her mouth and her spray of juices was still wet on his boots.

And then she knew she would be moving on again.

Chapter Thirteen

"Freddy's Place" was a BDSM club built mainly out of partition walls where regular sex cabarets were held. The club had been constructed inside a modern barn of pre-cast reinforced concrete beams and corrugated panels. For brief periods, Angela was actually permitted to see the world outside the barn and breathe the open-air. She knew that outwardly, it appeared to be a perfectly innocent farm building in the middle of some fields. Where the farm was actually situated, Angela of course had no idea. It made no difference to her life; that was to say, Crystal's life. What did a hot potato care about the location of the hands that juggled it about, savouring its warmth and taking little bites from it, and then passing it on? She was never in one place long enough to form any attachments.

But this was the place she had been kept for the longest time, even if that was only measured in days. Perhaps Freddy would keep her to the end, when she became too hot to handle. Maybe this would be her last ordeal. And then? Would she be returned to the real world?

She was certainly going out in exuberantly slavish fashion. She had been exposed to more people here than anywhere else, even at Jack and Jill's slave ball. There she had given a couple of impromptu performances. Here she was one performer in a carefully planned programme of slavish entertainment. She shrieked in pain and then sobbed in delight. She hated what they did to her and then she wanted more of it. Both extremes were intense and real, and she was trapped between them.

She was on stage again now…

* * *

Crystal was strapped spread-eagled to a cartwheel with a short axel extending behind it that was supported by a

131

heavy stand that held it at an angle so the wheel was tilted backwards. An electric motor turned the wheel once every ten seconds. As it turned, her heavy breasts flopped sideways and then seemed to crawl up her chest as she was inverted and then flopped back again. There were spiked weights clipped to her nipples which rotated about the domes of her breasts as the wheel did, endlessly pricking out circles in her soft flesh.

She had a rubber bit clenched between her teeth about which she dribbled and slobbered. The saliva and spittle spread across her face as she was turned head over heels; flowing into her eyes and hair as well as falling, along with her hot tears, onto her blazing breasts.

Padding over the hub of the wheel pressed into the small of her back and added tension to her body even as it lifted her hips outwards, making an inviting target of her groin. Her naked pussy was swollen and flushed pink and it also dribbled freely over her thighs and even, when she was inverted, up across her belly into her navel.

Two of the club's whip men stood on either side of the wheel lashing her body with electric spanking paddles and whips. They cracked audibly against her flesh and flashed and sparked as they drove electric needles deep into her. Her breasts flattened and shivered and her stomach clenched and her thighs rippled as the sparking paddles and sinuous thongs thwacked against them.

There were big screens on each side of the stage fed by images from cameras that showed every detail of her suffering in close up. The audience drank it in and clapped and cheered her suffering, and then brayed for more. And, helplessly, she gave it to them.

A whip thong slashed up between her spread thighs and rasped through her dribbling pussy cleft and across her hard clitoris. The jolt of pain it delivered was intense and overwhelming. Her bladder cut loose, as it had so many times before in a final show of humiliation and surrender, and a jet of hot pee spurted out between her sore lips across the stage.

Of course, as she was being rotated, the jet became a glistening arc that spurted up above her as she was inverted and fell like rain across her beaten, ravaged, trembling body, stinging as it flowed over her hot flesh. It was as if she had baptised her own degradation.

The cheers of the crowd almost brought the roof down.

The wheel was stopped with Crystal upright once more. But her performance was not over yet…

One of the whip men brought Fifi out on stage.

Of course, "Fifi" was not her real name any more than "Crystal" was Angela's. But it seemed appropriate for this slender, nervous, black girl with large round eyes and high perfect breasts. She was a perfect obedient little pet. The whip man led her by a leash clipped to her collar, while she shuffled after him on all fours like a puppy. The coffee coloured moons of her perfectly rounded bottom wiggled as she moved.

Fifi was positioned on her knees on the rubber tiles of the stage still splattered with Crystal's pee, with her bottom facing the audience and her face in Crystal's groin. The whip man pulled her hands up so that she grasped the spokes of the cartwheel and he cuffed them in place. A small flap in the front of the stage between Fifi's feet opened and a twin-pronged electric dildo on a telescopic amount extended an angle up towards the centre of the cartwheel. It penetrated Fifi's pussy and anus first of course. Her darker elastic flesh was spread and stretched about the prongs as they embedded themselves deep inside her. The pressure lifted her up so that her nose rubbed into Crystal's hot cleft.

LED lights built into the base of the dildo prongs flashed as a jolt of electricity was delivered into Fifi's insides.

She yelped in pain even as her tight passageways clenched about the dildo prongs. Convulsively she jerked forward and ground her face against Crystal's crotch. Her tongue slid out and began to lap and suck at her wet cleft, driven on by another jolt of pain. Crystal groaned and bit on her gag bar.

Her pee had only just preceded her cum. Once again, pain and shame had brought her to the brink of orgasm. Fifi would finish that in an appropriately shameful manner: tongued out by another naked slave girl in front of so many watching eyes.

Fifi was passionate, driven on by the jolt of electricity which came at steadily decreasing intervals. She was riding the prongs even as they tormented her, like a doe eyed masochist.

Crystal looked down her sweaty, beaten body just as Fifi raised her eyes to her: the whites showing starkly in her dark pretty face. She realized that at this precise moment they were both helpless to be or do anything else.

A monstrous orgasm overwhelmed Crystal and she sprayed her juices over Fifi's face. At the same moment she saw Fifi's face screw up in delight as she gasped and sprayed out her own juices over the cruel prongs of the dildo on which she was impaled.

The audience cheered and applauded their mutual, intimate and very public humiliation.

Crystal thought Fifi's pleasure was genuine. She hoped so. It was their only reward for suffering. But was it enough? Was it ever enough when they always, helplessly, wanted more?

Crystal was taken down from the cartwheel while Fifi was lifted off her impaling dildo. With a whip man holding both of them by their collars, they took their bows. And then came the final humiliation...

They turned their backs and bowed low with their legs spread, their heads hung low looking back between their knees at the audience. Then they reached behind them and pulled their elastic wet pussies wide.

A shower of coins was flicked at them. Some struck their buttocks and thighs, but others popped into their wet sex mouths and slid down into the tunnels of their vaginas, where they squeezed tight about them, holding them inside.

They gasped and yelped as they were rewarded so intimately. They were allowed to buy treats with all the tip money they could keep inside them…

The shower of coins ceased. They stood up, conscious of the metal jingling inside their pussies, and the whip man began to lead them offstage…

And then there was a sudden commotion in the audience. Voices rose in argument. There were angry shouts and suddenly punches were being exchanged. The whip man let go of Crystal and Fifi as he turned and jumped down from the stage into the audience try to sort the problem out.

Fifi simply stood where he had left her; unmoving, watching the fight with wide-eyed fascination. But Angela suddenly thought: I can leave now…

Calmly she walked off into the wings and down the steps into the backstage corridor. Distracted by the fight in the audience, there was nobody there to stop her. One side of the corridor was formed by the back wall of the barn. Half way along it was a bolted door that she knew led to the outside. She opened it and stepped through.

Cool night air enfolded her. She was in the pen at the back of the barn built on the apron concrete that surrounded it. It was where the girls were exercised and had been her only view of the outside world for several days. It was surrounded by a wire mesh fence which was not climbable with cuffed hands and hobbled feet. But she was only wearing her house collar. She could simply climb over it…

She did so.

She was free! She was dizzy with relief. Suddenly she could think again. Crystal faded away and now Angela was in charge once more.

Angela ran across the empty farmyard until she reached another fence. On the other side was an open fallow field bounded by a line of trees. She clambered over the fence and ran across the field, feeling the wild dew wet grass splashing about her bare feet. In a minute she had vanished between the trees, leaving Freddy's place far behind her.

* * *

The trees proved to be the edge of a rambling wood through which Angela cautiously picked her way for twenty minutes. Then it ended on the edge of a country lane that was totally deserted this time of night - which was perhaps just as well since she was totally naked. But she could see a light a little way along it. She jogged towards it and it turned out to be an old-fashioned red public phone box.

She pulled the door open and stepped inside. She saw the address of the box on the call information panel. She was on the Dimsford road, about 20 miles from home. She could call for help. She even had coins in her pussy! It was only right that the money paid for its use should buy her way back to freedom.

Then she shook her head. She did not need money to dial 999 and ask for the police. That was who she was going to call, wasn't it? Because she wanted the nightmare to be over, so she could get back home to where she was safe. She could wear clothes again and go back to normal life... and then?

What did she mean by *and then*?

What could take the place of what she had experienced over the last few weeks? And how could she tell her friends and family? The thought of the shame and their pity terrified her. No, she could not just go back to the way things had been. But she couldn't stay here all night dithering either. People from Freddy's might find her at any moment. They did own her, after all…

No, no, no! She was free now, she must not forget that.

Are you, Crystal asked?

Yes!

Then make a decision. You just have to dial the right number…

But what was right or wrong anymore?

Chapter Fourteen

The Flogger watched "The Deliverymen," as he knew them, put a limp Crystal into her carry crate, prior to loading her into their plain van parked outside his house. They were big men with their long hair tied back in pony tails and they looked surprisingly neat in their uniform blue overalls.

The carry crate was a rectangular waist high wooden box, square across its sides and top, but only half as deep. It had been laid on its back with its front open revealing a padded interior with many loops of rubber strapping fitted to it. Crystal was laid in it on her back, with their head brushing the top of the crate and her simmering bottom pressing against its base. It looked as though it had been built exactly to fit her. Straps went about her neck and waist, her arms were bent back and up and her hands were tucked into the top corners of the box and her wrists were fastened to its sides. A ball gag was pushed into her mouth. Her legs were bent and folded down into the crate so that her feet rested on the base of the box. Straps went about her ankles. Then her thighs were turned outward so they were almost flat against the back of the crate, exposing her still dribbling pussy and the pucker of her anus. Straps fitted to the back of the box went across her thighs and calves, holding them in place.

The lid of the crate was closed up and locked. Two of the Deliverymen then tilted it back up onto its base. There were rope handles on its sides so they could carry easily between them. You would never know what it contained, the Flogger thought, except for the ventilation holes drilled in its sides.

As Crystal was carried off, the Flogger handed over an envelope of cash to the chief Deliveryman.

'Where did you find a woman like that?' he asked.

The Deliveryman grinned. 'The first time was just business, the second time we got an offer we could not refuse…'

* * *

In the back of the van, as it made its way home, the chief Deliveryman sat beside Crystal's crate, which was resting on a wooden bench screwed to the wall. He was counting the cash the Flogger had given him. He put a portion away in his wallet and the rest he folded up into a small clear plastic sandwich bag, which he then rolled up tight and secured with an elastic band.

He opened the front of the crate. Crystal looked as though she was dozing in an exhausted sleep. He grinned and stuffed the roll of money up into her aching soiled pussy. She groaned and started and blinked foolishly.

He pulled out her gag and gave her drink from a water bottle.

'Two more bookings for you next week,' he said. '"The Headmaster" again, then a new woman calling herself "Mistress Boots"'.

'Thanks, Big Red,' Angela said wearily.

* * *

A few months before, in the early morning on the Dimsford Road, the bikers had pulled up beside a red telephone box. They looked around them in confusion. Big Red consulted Angela's telephone once again. 'The message said: *Pick up your hot potato from here for free. Bring spare leathers and a helmet.* Well, this is the spot.'

'It's not a police trap is it?' Mellow asked anxiously. 'I mean, who else knew that number?'

Just then Angela, still stark naked, stepped out from the shelter of the small copse behind the telephone box.

'I did, of course,' she said as they goggled at her in disbelief. 'After I escaped from Freddy's place, I realized that the only number I could ring was mine.'

'You rang us?' Big Red said.

'Of course. Is your computer still doing it stuff? Has anybody missed me yet?'

'No.'

'That's good. Now, if you can give me something to wear and take me back to wherever you hid my car, then I can go back home from my holiday and you won't have the police after you for real for kidnapping, rape, assault... you know the list.'

The bikers looked from one to the other in evident confusion and then back at her again.

'You aren't going to report us?' Big Red asked cautiously. 'What's got into you?

Angela laughed and ran a suggestive finger up through her bare pussy cleft. 'Oh, so many things have got into me, Big Red! But if you want to talk let's get off the road in case somebody comes by...'

And she disappeared behind the telephone box again.

The four motorbikes plunged after into the copse, pushing their way through the screen of bushes until they came upon her leaning casually back against a tree. The bikers surrounded her. They kicked down the supporting struts of their machines and turned their engines off.

Four bikers and her by a country lane, Angela thought. The way it started: but this time it would start afresh on her terms...

Big Red stepped forward and took hold of her by her hair. She did not resist. 'Explain,' he said.

'You created Crystal and she's part of me now,' Angela said calmly. She had had the night to think this through and now she understood. 'You could say I had to become a BDSM addict to survive BDSM. And now she's got to be fed. You were right. Cool, calm and collected Angela Winston could never admit what she secretly enjoyed. She had to be made to do it so that Crystal could take over. Now we need to be handled in

140

the right way...' She spread her legs. 'Are you up to it, or have you gone soft since I last saw you?'

'Soft!' Big Red roared.

True and Mellow pulled Angela's arms back around the sides of the tree and chained her wrists behind it, while Mean wrapped another chain across her neck and pulled it round the tree trunk, lifting her head up. In a few seconds she was helpless again. Red slapped her breasts and then opened his flies and rammed his cock into her. She sighed as the chains cut into her flesh and her bare buttocks were ground against the rough bar. How she missed this! It must have been all of six hours...

'That's right,' she gasped as he pumped into her, 'you can all have a dip into my money pot... as long as you smarten yourselves up first.'

She had them totally baffled now: helpless and yet somehow in command.

'What? Why?' Big Red spluttered as he screwed her.

'So you can be Crystal's roadies, of course. A hot potato must be delivered in style!'

THE END

Lightning Source UK Ltd.
Milton Keynes UK
UKHW020633290121
377903UK00011B/901